Blood Brothers

ANNE McALLISTER
and LUCY GORDON

Published by Silhouette Books

America's Publisher of Contemporary Romance

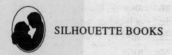 SILHOUETTE BOOKS

ISBN 0-373-76307-7

BLOOD BROTHERS

Visit Silhouette at www.eHarlequin.com

Printed in U.S.A.

Dear Reader,

Two years ago on a cold damp night in Bath, England, the two of us were sitting in a restaurant talking—as writers are wont to do—about *what if…*

What if we wrote a book together…what if we each had a hero…what if one was British and the other American…?

Of course, one *what if* led to another, and when Anne went home to America and Lucy went home to Northampton, we e-mailed each other more *what if*s…and Gabe and Randall—and their crusty grandfather, the earl—were born.

What we've written is a book about two men who look alike but think differently, cousins from opposite sides of the Atlantic, cast adrift in each other's world, floundering until two feisty, loving women take them in hand.

We wrote the Prologue and Epilogue jointly. Individually, Anne wrote about Gabe and Frederica (and counted on Lucy for advice on "darkest" Devon) and Lucy wrote about Randall and Claire (and depended on Anne to get her unscathed through a Montana winter).

Working together was a fresh and fun experience. We had a great time. We hope you do, too.

Anne McAllister   Lucy Gordon

Books by Anne McAllister

Silhouette Desire

*Cowboys Don't Cry #907
*Cowboys Don't Quit #944
*Cowboys Don't Stay #969
*The Cowboy and the Kid #1009
*Cowboy Pride #1034
*The Cowboy Steals a Lady #1117
*The Cowboy Crashes a Wedding #1153
*The Stardust Cowboy #1219
*A Cowboy's Secret #1279
Blood Brothers #1307

Silhouette Special Edition

*A Cowboy's Tears #1137

*Code of the West

Silhouette Books

World's Most Eligible Bachelors
*Cowboy on the Run

ANNE McALLISTER

RITA Award-winning author Anne McAllister fell in love with a cowboy when she was five years old. Tall, dark, handsome lone-wolf types have appealed to her ever since. "Me, for instance," her college professor husband says. Well, yes. But even though she's been married to the man of her dreams for over thirty years, she still likes writing about those men of the West! And even though she may take a break from cowboy heroes now and then, she has lots more stories planned for CODE OF THE WEST. She is always happy to hear from readers, and if you'd like, you can write to Anne at P.O. Box 3904, Bozeman, Montana 59772. SASE appreciated.

LUCY GORDON

met her husband-to-be in Venice, fell in love the first evening and got engaged two days later. They're still happily married and now live in England with their three dogs. For twelve years Lucy was a writer for an English women's magazine. She interviewed many of the world's most interesting men, including Warren Beatty, Richard Chamberlain, Sir Roger Moore, Sir Alec Guinness and Sir John Gielgud.

In 1985 she won the *Romantic Times* Reviewers' Choice Award for Outstanding Series Romance Author. She has also won a Golden Leaf Award from the New Jersey Chapter of RWA, was a finalist in the RWA Golden Medallion contest in 1988 and won the 1990 RITA Award in the Best Traditional Romance category for *Song of the Lorelei*.

In darkest Devon...
GABE

Prologue

As Gabe McBride's plane touched down in England he didn't have a clue that he was about to have a meeting with Destiny.

His cousin, Lord Randall Stanton, waiting for him outside Customs, didn't look like Destiny. Randall looked, as he always had, like an English version of Gabe: same tall figure and broad shoulders, same dark hair and eyes, and lean, handsome features that had a strong family likeness. Their differences lay less in looks than mannerisms.

Randall carried his head with the proud air of an English toffee.

"You'd know he was a lord, just looking at him," Gabe thought with an inward grin.

His own "air" suggested something entirely different. Generally it was one part horse, one part leather, one part bull rope rosin and several parts substances that polite society didn't talk about. At the moment he'd done his best to scrub all that away. No sense walking into the drawing room smelling like a barn.

Drawing room! Now there was a term he didn't use often. Didn't reckon he'd said it aloud since the last time he was here—and that had been fifteen years ago. The very notion made him smile, a drawing room was such a far cry from the homely lived-in clutter of the Montana ranch he called home—when he *was* home.

Usually he wasn't.

Usually he was going down the road from rodeo to rodeo. He'd be doing it now if it hadn't been for getting hung up on that little spinning bull at the National Finals in Vegas last month.

"Shoulder separation," the doc had said. "Again." He'd looked at Gabe over the top of his glasses. "How many is that?"

"Five," Gabe had admitted.

He didn't like to think about it even now. Didn't like to think about the surgery that had become inevitable, the months of recovery that would follow, the enforced idleness. A guy could get into trouble if he didn't have something to keep him busy. A guy could meet a girl like Tracy...

Even now his mouth curved instinctively at the thought of Tracy. He'd known she was trouble from the moment he saw her, but that was how he liked 'em. Trouble, and sassy and all woman. She'd lured him into her bed, with no resistance from him, and had cost him a fortune in gee-gaws, which was fine.

It was her uptight brother with the shotgun who hadn't been fine. Nor had the lively conversation they'd had in which the words "marriage", "honest woman" and "decent thing" had occurred with alarming frequency.

Gabe, who had been taught from the cradle never to bad-mouth a woman, didn't say that the words "honest" and "decent" were not exactly terms he would have used to describe Tracy. He'd just done his damnedest to assure the shotgun-toting brother that Tracy wouldn't want to tie herself to a no-account bull rider with no more morals than a monkey. And then he'd promised to hightail it out of the country so she could find herself a "respectable" man.

Gabe wished all the respectable men in the good ol' U.S. of A. the best of luck. He was off to visit his kin on the other side of the world.

That would keep him out of harm's—and Tracy's—way, and besides, it had the added benefit of pleasing his mother who couldn't go because she was just recovering from the flu and Martha, his sister, who was spending the semester abroad in Brazil.

In fact, Gabe was rather looking forward to a brief vacation visiting his English relatives—especially his mother's father, Earl Stanton, who was about to celebrate the fact that, in Randall's words, "Someone let the old devil live to be eighty, without strangling him."

But Destiny? Who needed it?

When you were young, healthy and in your prime, when there were always more ladies besides Tracy eager for your company, and you had enough money to indulge yourself, you made your own Destiny.

Which went to show how wrong a man could be!

Lord Randall Stanton broke into a grin at the sight of his scapegrace cousin loping out of the Customs Hall, and let out a yell that sat oddly with his elegant tailoring. It was met by an answering yell from Gabe, and for a moment the two young men pounded each other like schoolboys.

"It's good to see you," Randall said. "Even if it did take a scandal to get you here."

"Don't know what you're talking about," Gabe declared innocently. "The old man's eightieth—family duty, etc., etc., etc.—"

Randall just grinned. "Your mother called Grandpa just as I was leaving. Your secrets aren't secrets any more."

Gabe groaned. "Can't trust 'em to keep their mouths shut, can you?"

"I'm sure Aunt Elaine is the soul of discretion. Usually. Wait until we're in the car, and you can tell all," Randall said.

Like hell he would. He and Randall might have shared a thousand secrets as boys, but when it came to women, Gabe drew the line. He followed Randall out to the parking garage, and whistled at the sight of Randall's silver-colored Rolls-Royce.

"Does this come from the ancient family fortunes, or did Stanton Publications pay for it?"

"Stanton Publications," Randall told him. "All the family estates do is soak up money. It's the firm that makes it." He settled behind the wheel and looked avidly at his cousin. "Come on. Give. All I know is, it's something to do with a floozie called Tracy."

Gabe cocked his head. "Do I detect a little envy in your voice, cuz?"

Randall scowled, then shifted his gaze to focus intently on fitting the key into the ignition. "Of course not."

"It's not a crime, you know. Every red-blooded male ought to meet a Tracy or two."

"Or twelve or twenty," Randall said drily. "Or have you had more than that?"

"Wouldn't you like to know?" Gabe grinned as he leaned back against the leather seat and flexed his shoulders. "You should have a few floozies in your life, bud. It would make you a better human being."

"Like you, I suppose?" Randall snorted.

Gabe shrugged negligently. "All work and no play makes Randall a dull boy."

"Better than all play and no work," Randall said firmly.

One of Gabe's dark brows lifted. "Just a little testy, are we?" he asked as Randall negotiated the narrow lanes of the parking garage.

"You'd be testy too if you had Earl breathing down your neck every minute of every day."

They called Cedric Stanton "Grandfather" to his face; they called him "the earl" when speaking about him to acquaintances; but they called him "Earl" behind his back because one summer in Montana when they were boys, an old camp cook had actually thought it was the old man's name and kept yelling, "Hey, Earl! Come an' get it, Earl!"

Now Gabe grinned. "Hey, that's Earl. Just tell him to buzz off."

Randall gave a short sharp laugh. "I'd as soon tell a pit bull to play nice."

"So buzz off yourself. I don't see any chain around your neck. Invisible leash, is it?"

Randall almost unconsciously tugged at his collar. "Feels like it sometimes." He didn't say anything else, just concentrated on the road. Morning traffic around Heathrow was a good excuse for silence. But in fact, he had to admit Gabe had touched a raw nerve.

The death of Randall's parents in a car crash when he was eight had made him heir to the earldom and all its rights and responsibilities. His fearsome grandfather had left him in no doubt that he expected both sides of the equation to be kept up. Randall had learned estate management so that he could run the ancient family domains. He'd loved that part of his life. But it hadn't been profitable. At least not profitable enough. He'd also needed the skills to run the publishing empire by which the Stantons stayed one step ahead of the game.

He enjoyed that work, too, but he hadn't bargained for it eating away so much of his life. He'd bowed his head to the burdens, but sometimes a voice whispered in his ear that there was more to life than this; that it would be great to toss his cap over the windmill and forget the duties for awhile.

And when he was with his charming, light-hearted, devil-may-care cousin, the whisper threatened to become a roar.

Now his hands tightened on the steering wheel, so slightly that only the sharp-eyed Gabe could have noticed.

"So when do we hear of your engagement?" Gabe asked him.

Randall's head jerked around. "What engagement?"

"To Lady Honoria, or Lady Serena or Lady Melanie Wicks-Havering, or whoever. Time you did your duty to the House of Stanton, my lad."

"Stop sounding like Earl," Randall said in a harassed voice.

Gabe laughed. "So you've evaded the pack so far? But how

long can the fox stay ahead? Tally Hoooo!'' Gabe's imitation
of a hunting cry was excruciating.

''If I had my hands free I'd ram something down your gul-
let,'' Randall muttered. ''We can't all flit from flower to flower
with no thought for tomorrow.''

''Like I said, the ol' green-eyed monster seems to have bit
you but good.''

''Go to hell, McBride!''

''Oh, I reckon I will,'' Gabe said cheerfully, and settled
back as if satisfied that he'd done his bit for international re-
lations.

Earl was looking older.

Of course Gabe had seen him last three years ago when the
old man had come to Montana for a month's visit. Then he'd
seemed spry and ageless, his thick shock of white hair framing
a relatively unlined face, his bright blue eyes brimming with
enthusiasm and his every word outlining some new plan—
mostly, Gabe remembered, ones that involved work for Randall.

But now he saw lines in the old man's face. He saw a faint
tremble in Earl's fingers when, at the eightieth birthday bash,
the old man had raised his glass at his grandsons' toast to
''eighty more years as adventure-filled as the last eighty.''

He saw that some day Earl wouldn't be around anymore.

But he also saw that it was just possible that Randall would
die first—of overwork.

Gabe had been in England two days, and while he'd spent
a fair amount of time with the earl, he'd barely seen his cousin
after Randall had dropped him off at Stanton House in Bel-
gravia and had left.

''Got to be in Glasgow for a meeting,'' Randall said apol-
ogetically. ''Catch you later.''

But he hadn't. Since Gabe's arrival, Randall had been var-
iously in London, Glasgow, Manchester, Cardiff and Pen-
zance. The most Gabe heard from him was a phone call or
another apologetic message. He barely even made it to Earl's
birthday bash.

He rang to say he'd be a bit late, and when he finally blew in, he stayed long enough for the toast and a piece of cake, and then he excused himself to make calls about a buyout.

Gabe, on the other hand, had a wonderful time. He discussed horseflesh with a couple of his grandfather's cronies, wrapped himself around a fantastic meal. He danced with all the pretty ladies—of whom there were plenty—and flirted with the prettiest of the lot—a stunning blonde called Natasha, who looked at him with big violet eyes and said, "You're not much like your cousin, are you?"

"Nope," Gabe replied cheerfully. "Thank God."

When the party finally ended, Randall still hadn't returned. He was probably off somewhere making more money for Stanton Publishing or stopping the cash from flowing out of the Stanton ancestral coffers.

Gabe glanced at his watch. "Have you ever considered giving him a day off?" He and the earl were in the library, cozily ensconced in deep leather chairs, quaffing the best single malt scotch Gabe had ever tasted, and Gabe thought the old man looked mellow enough to allow him to consider broaching the subject.

"Day off?" Earl snorted. "Day *off?* Nobody ever gave *me* a day off! Earls don't get days off."

Gabe smiled thinly. Poor old Randall. "Reckon I'm glad I'm just a lowly commoner then." He raised his glass in toast. "To the rabble. Long may we loaf."

Earl made a harrumphing sound. "You needn't be so almighty proud of it, my lad. Most men, by your age, have something to show for their lives."

"You, for instance?" Gabe knew damned well the old man had been a wastrel in his salad days. It had taken a very determined Lady Cornelia Abercrombie-Jones to take Cedric David Phillip Stanton in hand, get a marriage proposal out of him and put an end to his frivolous ways.

"We aren't talking about me," Earl said huffily.

"You're not," Gabe agreed, "because you know it will undercut your case. I don't care that you were a hellion. In fact, I'm all for it, as you know." He grinned. "I just think

you ought to allow Randall a shot at a little hell-raising—
before you croak and make sure he never gets a day off.''

''You think I'm about to stick my spoon in the wall?''

''Does that mean die? No, probably not. But someday
you're going to. And if Randall hasn't lived, who can tell what
he might do with the Stanton legacy, with all those 'burdens'
and 'responsibilities' you keep loading on him. He might just
throw it all away!''

Earl's face turned bright red. ''Randall would never—!''

''How do you know? Have you ever let him out past ten
o'clock? Except on business?''

Gabe never heard the answer to that question because the
next moment the library door opened and Randall returned. A
satisfied smile lit his often sober face. ''We've done it. We've
got the *Gazette*!''

''Another *Gazette*?'' Gabe groaned. ''How many *Gazettes,
Echoes, Advertisers, Recorders* and whatever else does that
make?''

Stanton Publishing specialized in local newspapers, and
owned eighty, all over the country.

''This is the *Buckworthy Gazette*,'' Randall said triumphantly. ''We've been after it for years.''

''Ah.'' Gabe nodded in comprehension. The family seat was
situated near the little town of Buckworthy, right down south
in the county of Devon. It had always galled the Stantons that
they couldn't get their hands on the paper for their own locality. Now, at long last, Randall had triumphed.

Earl, of course, was over the moon. He leapt from his chair,
rejuvenated, and slapped his grandson on the back, hollering
his delight. ''About time! Another few months and it would
have gone right down the drain. Now you can turn it around,
make it shine.'' He glanced at his watch. ''If you leave early
enough tomorrow you can be down there by midday. It's a
Thursday paper. You'll be in time to have some input on this
week's issue. No time like the present to begin putting things
to rights. Sales haven't been what they should be. You can
start up an advertising campaign, too. And some sort of
weekly contest. The one you did in Thrush-by-the-Marsh

worked like a charm. Something like that!'' Earl rubbed his hands together in glee.

But as Gabe watched, the enthusiasm seemed to drain right out of Randall, as if it were being choked off. As it probably was—by the added tug on the noose of even greater responsibilities.

''Whoa. Hey, hold up. You'll choke him!'' He looked at Randall and slid a finger around the inside of his collar.

Randall hesitated. His hand crept up and loosened his tie. His mouth opened. And closed again. He didn't say a word.

Idiot! Gabe glared at him. Was he going to let the old man run him into the ground? Randall glared back.

Earl looked from one to the other of them. He frowned. ''What's the problem?''

''No problem,'' Randall said at the same moment Gabe said, ''Big problem! Here you go pushing more work off on him! I just told you, he needs a break!''

''And I told you there's work to be done!''

''Get someone else!''

''*Someone else?*'' Earl sounded as if he couldn't believe his ears. He was working himself up, breathing hard and going red in the face. ''*The Buckworthy Gazette* is the Stanton paper,'' he roared. ''Ours by right. And failing badly. It's going to take a Stanton to turn it around.''

''But why does it have to be this Stanton?'' Gabe demanded.

''Because Martha is on the other side of the world.''

''*Martha* is not the only other Stanton!''

''Well, no, there's you,'' Earl said witheringly, ''I'd as soon ask a fourteen-year-old to run a bank as send you to turn the *Gazette* around!''

''You don't think I can do it?''

''It's work,'' Earl pointed out.

''You don't think it's work to raise cattle? You don't think it's work to sort and ship and doctor a herd?''

''Your father worked hard,'' Earl allowed.

Big of him! Gabe gritted his teeth. ''I worked with him!''

''You lent a hand when you passed by.''

"Who do you think did it since Dad died last year?"

"You?" Earl almost seemed to chuckle. "I thought that's why your mother hired Frank as foreman. Or maybe Martha did it or that little orphan girl, Claire. Your mother says she lives in jeans and does the work of three men. Who needs you?"

Gabe's teeth came together with a snap. "Think again."

"You don't say you're actually good for a job of work, surely?" Earl regarded him with tolerant amusement.

"I'm good for anything *he's* good for," Gabe snapped, indicating Randall.

"Ho, ho, ho!" Earl scoffed.

"Don't ho-ho me, old man—"

"And don't call me old man—"

"Look—" Randall ventured.

As one, the other two turned on him. "YOU KEEP OUT OF IT!"

"Whatever needs to be done, I'll do it," Gabe said defiantly. "And *you*—" to Randall "—give me the details of this paper, and go take a vacation. Or 'a holiday,' I suppose you'd call it."

"What I'd call it is madness." Randall shook his head fiercely. "You'll bankrupt us."

Gabe slammed his glass down on the table. "Sez who? You think I can't run things? I'll show you. I'm off to Devon in the morning!"

There was silence.

Randall and Earl looked at each other. Then at Gabe.

Gabe glared back at them. And then, just as the adrenaline rush carried him through an eight-second bull ride mindless of aches, pains and common sense, before it drained away, so did the red mist of fury disperse and the cold clear light of reality set in.

And he thought, *oh hell, what have I done?*

Slowly, unconsciously, he raised a hand and ran his finger around the inside of the collar of his own shirt.

* * *

Much later the cousins put Earl to bed, then supported each other as far as Gabe's room, where he produced a bottle of Jack Daniel's.

"Seriously," Randall said, "it's a crazy idea…"

"Yep, it is." Gabe poured them each a glass and lifted his. "To the *Buckworthy Gazette*!"

"You don't have to do—"

"Yes," Gabe said flatly. "I do." He downed the whisky in one gulp, then set the glass down with a thump and threw himself down onto his bed to lie there and stare up at his cousin. Randall looked a little fuzzy.

Gabe felt a little fuzzy, but determined. "Seriously," he echoed his cousin. "Remember when we were kids and you came to Montana for the first time. We became blood brothers, swearing to defend and protect each other against all comers. Well, that's exactly what I'm doing."

Randall shook his head. "I don't need protecting!"

Gabe wasn't convinced, but he wasn't going to argue. He shoved himself up against the headboard of the bed and reached for the bottle again. Carefully he poured himself another glass, aware of Randall's tight jaw, his cousin's years of hard work and legendary determination.

"There's another thing, too. You're not the only Stanton," he muttered.

Randall blinked. "What?"

Gabe looked up and met his cousin's gaze. "I can do this." Though, as he said the words, Gabe wondered if he was saying them for Randall's ears or for his own. "It will be fun," he added after a moment with a return of his customary bravado.

"But you don't know what you're getting into."

Gabe held up his glass and watched the amber liquid wink in the light.

"That," he said, "is exactly why it's going to be fun."

One

How hard could it be?

Gabe was determined to look on the positive side. There was no point, after all, in bemoaning his impulsive decision. He'd said he would do it, and so he would. No big deal.

Randall apparently did this sort of thing all the time— dashed in on his white horse—no, make that, sped in in his silver Rolls-Royce—and rescued provincial newspapers from oblivion, set them on their feet, beefed up their advertising revenues, sparked up their editorial content, improved their economic base and sped away again—just like that.

Well, fine. Gabe would, too. No problem. No problem at all.

The problem was finding the damn place!

Gabe scowled now as he drove Earl's old Range Rover through the gray morning drizzle that had accompanied him from London, along the narrow winding lane banked by dripping hedgerows taller than his head.

He'd visited the ancestral pile before, of course, but he'd

never driven himself. And he'd always come in the middle of summer, not in what was surely the dampest, gloomiest winter in English history.

He'd left way before dawn this morning, goaded by Earl having said something about Randall always getting "an early start." He'd done fine on the motorway, despite still having momentary twitches when, if his concentration lapsed, he thought he was driving on the wrong side of the road.

It had almost been easier when he'd got down into the back country of Devon and the roads had ceased having sides and had become narrow one-lane roads. His only traumas then came when he met a car coming in the other direction and he had to decide which way to move. Finally though, he found a sign saying BUCKWORTHY 3 mi and below it STANTON ABBEY 2 mi.

He turned onto that lane, followed it—and ended up on a winding track no wider than the Range Rover.

He felt like a steer on its way to the slaughterhouse—funneled into a chute with no way out.

And there was an apt metaphor for you, he thought grimly.

The lane twisted again, the hedgerows loomed. The windshield wipers swept back and forth, condensation rose. Gabe muttered under his breath.

Where were the wide-open spaces when you needed them?

"Damn!" He rounded the next blind curve and found himself coming straight up the rear tire of an antiquated bicycle that wobbled along ahead of him.

He swerved. There was no time to hit the brakes. The rider swerved at the same time—fortunately in the opposite direction.

Gabe breathed again as he passed, leaving the bicyclist, who appeared to be an elderly woman swaddled in a faded red sweater over more clothes than were necessary to get through a Montana winter, staring after him, doubtless unnerved, but fortunately unscathed.

It wouldn't have done to have flattened a local.

"I thought you intended to *save* the *Gazette,* not make headlines in it," he could well imagine Earl saying sarcastically.

Earl had openly scoffed when Gabe had proposed to take care of things and be back in a week.

"*A week?* You think you're going to turn ten years worth of sliding sales, bad management and terrible writing around in *a week?*"

"Well, two, then," Gabe had muttered. How the hell was he supposed to know? He'd never saved a newspaper before. He barely even read them—beyond checking the price of steers and maybe glancing at the sports page.

"Two months," Earl had said loftily. "If you're clever."

Two *months?* Gabe had stared. "I have to be back for calving and branding come spring!" he protested.

"Guess you'll have to leave it to Randall then," Earl had said with a bland smile.

Like hell he would!

He'd said he would rescue the *Gazette.* And damn it, he would. No matter how long it took.

He knew Randall, too, thought he'd blow it. He'd spent half the night before Gabe left giving him advice. "Just go in there and lay down the law. Speak authoritatively."

"Be the lord and master, you mean?" Gabe said derisively.

"Exactly. Speak softly but carry a big stick."

"Teddy Roosevelt said that."

Randall blinked. "Did he? Well, he must have stolen it from us." Then he'd clapped Gabe on the shoulder. "You'll be fine. Everything will be right as rain if you just…well, no matter. If you can't, you just ring me up."

"No, I can't," Gabe said smugly. "You'll be in Montana."

That was the other part of the deal. Gabe would do his job if Randall would oversee the ranch.

"Nothing to it," Gabe had reassured his cousin, though Randall hadn't looked all that cheerful at the prospect. "Piece of cake."

And this would be, too, he assured himself. And if it wasn't, he'd get it done anyway. He'd show both Earl and Randall. He was tired of having everybody think he couldn't last at anything for longer than eight seconds.

But one look at Stanton Abbey when he finally found it, and Gabe thought if he made eight seconds he'd be lucky.

He'd last visited Stanton Abbey when he was ten. He was thirty-two now. It hadn't changed. Of course, twenty-two years in the life of Stanton Abbey was a mere blink of an eye.

The original building was seven hundred years old if it was a day. There had been additions over the years. The damp dark stone building sat on the hillside like a squat, stolid Romanesque stone toad with slightly surprised gothic eyebrows.

The surprise no doubt came in part from having had a Tudor half-timbered extension grafted onto one side and a neo-classical wing tacked onto the other. Since the eighteenth century nothing had been added, thank heavens. The upkeep on what was already there had kept two hundred years of Stantons busy enough.

Gabe had never really envied Randall the earldom. His first adult look at Stanton Abbey gave him no reason to change his opinion. In fact he wondered that Randall hadn't said, "Thanks, but no thanks," long ago.

When he was ten, Gabe had thought Stanton Abbey an endlessly fascinating place. He and Randall had chased each other down long stone corridors, had hidden from Earl in the priest's hole and had raced to see who could first get through the garden maze.

Anyone who ventured into the garden now, Gabe thought as he stared at the brambles and bushes, had better mark a trail or he'd never be seen again.

Randall had tried to warn him.

"It's a bit overgrown," he'd said. "We keep up with the house. Got to, you know. It's a listed building, grade one, and all that. And Freddie's done a wonderful job with the renovations. Still, every time I go down it seems some timbers need replacing—and there's been a spot of bother with the rising damp."

Rising?

Drowning, more like. Gabe could feel it permeating his bones. Had he really committed himself to living here for the next two months?

In a word, yes. And he wasn't about to turn tail and run.
Earl would never let him live it down.

Well, if Randall could do it, so could he.

He'd just find Freddie the caretaker to let him in.

Frederica Crossman was not expecting visitors.

That was why she was still in her nightgown and down on
her hands and knees on the stone-flagged floor of Stanton Abbey's dower house at ten o'clock on Monday morning, trying
to coax her son Charlie's on-loan-from-school-over-the-
Christmas-holidays rabbit out from under the refrigerator.

Charlie was supposed to have taken it with him, but he
hadn't managed to catch it before he left for school this morning.

"It absolutely has to be back today, Mum," he'd told her,
"or I'm toast."

"I'll catch him," Freddie had promised blithely at ten
minutes to eight. She'd been trying ever since.

Now she could almost reach the little creature. If only she
had longer fingers…or the rotten bunny wasn't terrified…or…

The knock on the door startled her. She jerked and banged
her head on the desk next to the refrigerator. "Blast!"

Another knock came, louder and more persistent than the
first.

Freddie didn't want to answer. She knew precisely who it
was—Mrs. Peek. Freddie had been expecting her ever since
she'd learned yesterday that Stanton Publishing had bought
The Gazette. Mrs. Peek, the village's most ardent gossip, was
bound to appear, eager for a cup of tea and the latest news.

Freddie was only surprised it had taken her so long.

When Lady Adelaide Bore, a member of another Family Of
Note in the neighborhood, had run off with her groom, Mrs.
Peek had known about it before the ink was dry on the fare-
well note.

A third imperious knock.

Irritably, Freddie pulled Charlie's old mac around her like
a dressing gown and, still rubbing the bump on her head,
opened the back door.

It wasn't Mrs. Peek.

It was a man. A lean, ruggedly handsome man with thick, ruffled dark hair and intense blue eyes. A memorable man.

Freddie remembered him at least. And she had no doubt that Mrs. Peek would, too.

It was Lord Randall Stanton. The *heir.*

Or was it? Suddenly Freddie wasn't sure.

Freddie had met Lord Randall Stanton two or three times when he'd brought his grandfather down for a visit to the ancestral home. Lord Randall had always been charming, solicitous, unfailingly polite. Very public school. All his tailoring bespoke. She couldn't imagine him being caught dead in blue jeans.

But blue jeans, faded and worn in exceedingly interesting places, were just what this man wore. Even more astonishing, he had a huge shiny gold object affixed to the center of his belt. A buckle? Freddie had seen serving platters that were smaller!

"Hi," he said and gave her the famous Stanton grin.

His American accent settled one issue. Whoever he was, he wasn't Lord Randall.

"Hello?" Freddie replied cautiously. She clutched Charlie's mac tightly around her.

The grooves at the corners of his smile deepened. "I'm Gabe McBride. I'm looking for the caretaker of Stanton Abbey. Is he in?"

"He?"

It was not one of Freddie's finer moments.

Caretakers were not always men. She suspected even the American Mr. McBride would be willing to admit that. But even he, she imagined, would expect a caretaker of either sex to be dressed by ten o'clock in the morning.

But before she could panic about that, she caught sight of the rabbit out of the corner of her eye as it dashed from beneath the refrigerator toward the old cooker. "'Scuse me!" Freddie exclaimed and plunged after it.

She expected Gabe McBride, obviously some relation to the

Stantons as his likeness marched up and down the portrait hall at the abbey, to stand by and watch her make a fool of herself.

She was astonished when he joined her.

"Is it a rat?" He was on his knees beside her, all eagerness, his dark hair shedding drops of rain on the flagstone floor.

She shook her head. "A bunny."

"A bunny? A *rabbit?*"

"Yes! Here, Cosmo! Cosmo, come here! There's a nice bunny. It's time for school, Cosmo." She was crawling on the floor, trying to stretch toward the back of the cooker where she could see the rabbit hunched, its beady left eye looking straight at her.

"I'll get it." Gabe McBride flopped down on his belly next to her. He scrabbled forward, reaching for the bunny who, seeing he was outnumbered, feinted left, looked right and skittered right between the two of them and ran into the dining room.

Freddie bit off a very unladylike exclamation, leapt to her feet and, still clutching the mac around her, ran after it with Gabe McBride in close pursuit.

"You go that way," he directed. "I'll go this." He jerked his head, directing her. "We'll head him off at the pass."

"I beg your pardon?"

He grinned. It was lethal.

It was a good job, Freddie thought, that she was on her knees already, else she'd be lying out flat on the flagstones that very minute. *And letting the man have his way with you.*

"Never!" she exclaimed aloud.

"What?" said Gabe McBride.

Freddie shook her head. "N-nothing. I was just saying we're *never* going to catch him."

"Sure we will. Just do what I told you." He edged around the other way. "Be real still. I'll flush him out toward you. Ready?"

Still reeling from her aberrant, wholly inappropriate thoughts, Freddie crouched, feeling like a goalkeeper at the ready, nightgown and mac draped around her.

Gabe McBride got on his belly again and stretched beneath

the china cabinet. The rabbit watched worriedly. Gabe's fingers got closer and closer.

"Yes," she breathed. "You're going to..."

Then all of a sudden, Gabe smacked his hands together in a loud clap. The rabbit shot out directly toward Freddie.

"Gotcha!" And she fell over on her rear end, clutching the rabbit gently in both hands. Her heart slammed against the wall of her chest.

From the exhilaration of the chase, she assured herself, *not* from the handsome American grinning down at her!

"Way to go!" He was breathing heavily, too, and his shirttails were pulled out and he had a button undone.

There came a knock. The door opened. "Yoo-hoo, m'dear?" called Mrs. Peek. "Anybody home?"

Freddie was a *girl!*

Well, actually she was a *woman*—and quite a woman at that, with her tumbling wavy dark hair and her flushed cheeks. Not to mention the womanly curves and heaving bosom Gabe had been treated to as they'd chased down the rabbit.

"I'm the caretaker," she told him breathlessly as she carried the rabbit to its cage.

"You're *Freddie?*"

"Frederica," she said firmly. "My husband worked for Earl Stanton." At his quizzical look she added, "Mark died four years ago."

This entire conversation took place in the scant moments it took for them to return to the kitchen, rabbit in tow, and intercept an elderly woman in a red sweater who was making herself at home in the kitchen. She was, Gabe realized, the one with the bicycle he'd almost mowed down in the lane.

She was looking from one to the other of them, blue eyes alight with curiosity.

"This is Mr. McBride. Mr. McBride, meet Mrs. Peek," Freddie-the-caretaker said briskly as she put the rabbit in the cage on the table.

Gabe nodded politely and shook the woman's hand, but his attention never strayed very far from the delectable Freddie.

He hadn't been able to keep his eyes off her since she'd opened the door to him wearing that ridiculous too-small raincoat over what looked to be a nightgown.

A soft flannel nightgown with sprigs of some kind of purple flowers on it such as, his fashion-conscious sister Martha would have said, only sexless grannies wore. Martha would have been wrong. Big time.

Gabe sucked in another careful breath.

"Have you got a pain, Mr. McBride?" Mrs. Peek asked.

"What?"

"You seems to be havin' trouble breathing."

Well, yes. But mostly he was having more trouble controlling what Earl would doubtless call "his baser nature."

Freddie-the-caretaker was enticing as all get out. Still, he didn't think his grandfather would look kindly on his throwing the resident caretaker down on the kitchen table and having his way with her. Especially not with the old lady in the red sweater avidly looking on.

Mrs. Peek, he decided after a few minutes' conversation, was very well named.

Nothing happened in the village of Buckworthy that Mrs. Peek didn't know about. She certainly knew about *him!*

"Come t'run the *Gazette*," she said, bobbing her head in approval. Then her brows arched behind her glasses and she looked from him to Freddie-the-caretaker with her loose hair and mussed nightgown and said, "And a mighty fast worker he is, too."

"Mr. McBride came for the keys to the abbey," Freddie said firmly. But while she contrived to sound firm and businesslike, her hands fluttered around, as if she was torn between smoothing her disheveled hair or clutching the raincoat even tighter.

As she was managing to do neither, Gabe just stood there and enjoyed the view. The prospect of spending two months in Devon was looking brighter all the time.

"Us could do with a cup of tea," Mrs Peek said.

Freddie put on the kettle.

Mrs. Peek smiled brightly. "You're the young lord's cousin, then? The American. Has the look of 'is lordship, he

does,'' she pronounced. "He were right han'sum, too. Th'
earl, I mean. Cedric." Mrs. Peek's voice softened and became
almost dreamy. Her cheeks were already red from the cold,
but if they hadn't been Gabe felt sure that the thought of Earl
might have contributed.

Earl? Make someone's heart beat faster? Now there was a
sobering thought.

"You know my grandfather, Mrs. Peek?"

The ruddy color on her cheeks deepened. She looked a little
flustered. "Us was…acquainted."

Gabe bet they were. And very well acquainted at that. Mrs.
Peek had to be seventy-five if she was a day, and it was a
little hard to imagine her and Earl getting it on. But then it
was a little hard imagining Earl once looking like him!

"I'll give him your regards when I talk to him," he said.
"I just came down from Stanton House where we celebrated
his birthday."

That, of course, required a detailed description of the birthday party. Mrs. Peek was all ears. Freddie, to Gabe's dismay,
excused herself after she'd poured the tea.

"I'll be right back," she said. "I just need to get
more…presentable." Her hands were fluttering still.

"Don't bother on my account," Gabe grinned.

Freddie clutched the raincoat across her midsection and said
firmly, "I'll be back in a few minutes."

"'Er's a dear soul, our Freddie," Mrs. Peek said the moment Freddie was out of earshot. "Always workin', 'er is. Too
much for one woman, keepin' up wi' the abbey, but can't tell
her so. Good job you've come. Right proper Stantons gettin'
the *Gazette* an' old Cedric sendin' his very own grandson to
set things right. As well he should," she said firmly. "This
bein' his old home, an' all. Th' neighborhood needs 'er gen-
tlemen."

Gabe looked over his shoulder, then realized the gentleman
in question was him! He began to feel a bit of the responsibility Randall seemed to shoulder so easily.

"I'll do my best."

Mrs. Peek nodded eagerly "You've got plans?"

"Have to see it first. Check things out. Assess the situation. Develop a plan of attack." He was pretty sure that was the sort of claptrap Randall would have come up with when pressed. "I'll know more in the next few days."

"That's for sure." Mrs. Peek smiled.

Gabe wasn't sure what she meant by that cryptic comment. She finished her cup of tea, then got up. "Glad you've come, me han'sum. Wish'ee well." Her blue eyes sparkled and Gabe had a glimpse of what Earl must have been drawn by all those years ago. Then, nodding with satisfaction, she added, "'Tis time."

She was pedaling down the drive when Freddie returned.

Her hair was pulled up and pinned on top of her head, and she was dressed now in jeans and a bright blue loose-necked pullover sweater. She wasn't quite as obviously delectable as she had been crawling around on the floor in her nightgown giving him a glimpse of long lovely legs, but Gabe had a good memory.

"Where's Mrs. Peek?"

"On her way. She got what she came for."

Freddie smiled. "She means well. She lives alone and she enjoys a cup of tea and a chat." Freddie swished through the kitchen, picking up the cups and putting them in the sink. The jeans hugged her hips and thighs. Not bad. Gabe watched them sway, then dragged his gaze upward and his mind back to the point.

He cleared his throat. "I get the feeling she thinks I'm here for good. I'm not." He wanted that clear right now. "I'm doing Randall...my cousin...a favor. I said I'd sort the *Gazette* out. I will. Then I'm gone. This is just a one-time deal. I have a ranch back in Montana. I'm a cowboy, not a lord."

"A cowboy?" Freddie said doubtfully, as if it were in a foreign tongue. Her lips curved. She had very kissable lips.

Gabe wondered what they would taste like.

Had Earl wondered the same thing about Mrs Peek's the first time he'd seen her? Had she been a pretty young thing, too?

Freddie wasn't that young, he reminded himself firmly. She

was a widow. She had kids old enough to go to school. That made her pretty old herself.

"How old are you?" he asked, unsure why he needed to know. He expected her to say forty or so. Mothers were. His own was nearly sixty, after all.

"Thirty-one."

"*Thirty-one?*"

She was younger than he was! Gabe stared at Frederica Crossman, poleaxed. "How old are your kids?" It wasn't a question as much as an accusation.

"Charlie's nine. Emma's seven."

Gabe opened his mouth. He closed it again, having nothing at all to say. She was thirty-one and her kids were *half grown!*

That meant *he* could have kids that old!

No. He couldn't!

He was barely more than a kid himself.

"It's not polite to ask someone's age," Freddie said tartly, "especially if you're going to stare at me dumbfounded when I give you an honest answer."

Gabe flushed. "Sorry. I didn't mean...I'm just...surprised. You look so...so *young*." He'd thought she was an incredibly well-preserved forty.

He shook his head, still trying to sort it out. He'd never thought about aging before. Not himself at least. Earl, yes. The old man was whiter and frailer, even though his voice still boomed and his spirit never flagged.

Randall, too, had aged. There were marked differences between the boy Randall had been at eighteen and the man he'd become.

But Gabe hadn't really thought it had anything to do with age. He'd just thought Randall looked old because he worked so damn hard.

Now he wasn't so sure.

Maybe they were all getting older. Earl at least had a life's work to look back on with pride. And Randall, too, had something to show for it. So apparently did Freddie Crossman, mother of two half-grown children.

What about him? What about Gabriel Phillip McBride?

He looked down at his bull-riding championship belt buckle. Suddenly it didn't seem like enough.

Two

She should have invited him to stay with them.

It would have been the polite thing, the responsible thing, certainly the financially sensible thing to do! After all, Freddie often opened the dower house to holidaymakers looking for a B&B.

But it wasn't summer. It was January, as cold and bleak and wintry as it ever got in Devon. Her favorite time of year because for once she had time for herself and Charlie and Emma.

Nothing said she *had* to open her home to Gabe McBride— just because she owed his grandfather more than she could ever repay.

He'd never asked for repayment. He'd never so much as hinted.

But Freddie knew she owed him. The earl felt guilty about the death of her husband, Mark, though she had assured him over and over it was Mark who'd made the decision to sail the earl's boat home that night; it was Mark who had taken the foolish risk; no one—least of all Lord Stanton—had commanded him to.

But the earl didn't see it that way.

"He was working for me," he said. "I take care of my own."

The feudal blood in Lord Stanton's veins ran deep. It didn't matter that Freddie was earning a living, albeit meager, as a renovator and could make ends meet. She and her children were, he informed her, his responsibility. He would see to their welfare. Next thing she knew he arranged for them to move from their little flat in Camden to the Stanton Abbey dower house.

"I don't know anyone in Devon!" she'd protested.

"You'll meet them."

"My business—"

"Will thrive. You renovate. Renovate the abbey."

"My children—"

"Can go to school in fresh air and have acres and acres to play in."

For every argument she had, the earl had had an answer. No one ever said no to the earl. Certainly Freddie never managed to.

So she was very grateful now that he *hadn't* asked her to put up his grandson!

She didn't know how she could have refused.

She only knew she would have had to!

Gabe McBride set off all the bells and whistles of attraction that Freddie was certain had well and truly died with Mark. It had been *four years* since Mark's death, and she hadn't once looked at another man.

But she had looked at Gabe McBride today.

Then she'd have handed him a key and sent him on his way. She wished she could have sent him clear back to America!

The feelings were all too familiar. The attraction all too strong. It was the same thing she'd felt for Mark.

And the very last thing she needed.

A *cowboy,* for heaven's sake!

She'd already proved her susceptibility to one handsome devil-may-care man—Mark had been wild and dashing and reckless. It didn't take much imagination to see that Gabe McBride, however much blue Stanton blood ran in his veins, was another red-blooded, risk-taking man.

She'd read his belt buckle, hadn't she? It had proclaimed him a Salinas bull-riding champion.

Freddie wasn't sure exactly what being a bull-riding champion was, but she was pretty sure it wasn't anything safe.

No, sorry. No matter how much she owed the earl, she wasn't offering hospitality to the likes of Gabe McBride.

Not a chance.

Gabe had always thought himself hale and hearty—resilient, capable of withstanding great extremes of weather. He was, after all, Montana born-and-bred.

He damn near froze his ass off in one night in Stanton Abbey!

"Get a good night's sleep," Earl had told him cheerfully when Gabe had rung before bedtime.

Sleep? Gabe doubted he slept a wink. He spent the whole day reacquainting himself with the Abbey and all night prowling the cupboards, looking for more blankets, piling them on, trying to sleep, shivering, then rising to go look for more.

He understood the meaning of "rising damp" now. It was what got you up to go find more covers.

Central heating had come along a good six hundred years after the abbey, and though it did its best, it couldn't rise to the occasion. The pipes hissed and moaned. They sputtered and rattled. Gabe turned it off again.

After all, he wasn't a sissy. He could cope.

He considered starting a blaze in a fireplace. But the fireplaces were big enough to roast an ox in. Gabe reckoned he'd have to move right in with the wood to get the benefit of any warmth. In the end, he piled on every piece of clothing he'd brought, buried himself beneath every blanket he could find, and huddled next to the stove for the night.

He was sure Earl would call it bracing.

He called it ridiculous. But he didn't seriously consider

other options until he drove past the cozy warmth of the dower house on his way to the *Gazette* office in the morning.

All of the dower house chimneys appeared to be working. He remembered the kitchen had been cheerful, not echoing, the parlor welcoming, not forbidding, and the occupant…well, he'd been thinking about her all night.

He cast a longing glance over his shoulder as he drove past—and noticed a discreet little sign at the end of the dower house drive.

B&B FULL BREAKFAST £15. DINNER AT EXTRA COST.

He smiled. "Well, now why didn't she mention that?"

Fixing the *Buckworthy Gazette* would best be accomplished, Gabe had decided by lunchtime, if he simply lobbed a bomb into the building, blew up the whole place.

Unfortunately that solution was out of the question.

"I say we set fire to it, throw 'em out on their ears, and start over," he told Earl when the old man rang up later that afternoon. "The place is falling down around their ears, and they don't give a rat's ass. There's not a computer in the building. The printing press looks like it came over on the May-flower—"

"We didn't go on the Mayflower," Earl reminded him. "We're still here."

"And they're still probably using the same damn one! I swear I saw a pen with a quill. I'm surprised there's a telephone."

"There wasn't," Earl said cheerfully, "last time I was there."

"When was that?" Gabe wanted to know. "Last week?"

"Tut-tut," Earl admonished. "Sarcasm won't get you anywhere with these people. They are fixtures—"

"You can say that again." Made of stone, if Gabe's first impression was accurate.

They had all assembled in the main room when he arrived—two reporters, a receptionist-cum-tea-lady, the printer and the office manager all lined up in a row and bowed and scraped and tugged their forelocks when he'd come in.

He'd been appalled, but, taking a page from Randall's book, had very firmly told them that things were about to change, that they were going to make a profitable paper out of the *Gazette* and he was going to tell them exactly how to do it.

"Yes, Mr. McBride."

"Quite so, Mr. McBride."

"Whatever you say, Mr. McBride."

"We need a computer," he told the office manager, Percy Pomfret-Mumphrey, a man as pompous and fussy as his name.

"A computer?" Percy squeaked.

"Software," Gabe went on relentlessly. "We'll need a database. A spreadsheet. We'll want to enter the subscription list. The advertisers. We can look into offset printing," he told John the printer. "And we need an answering machine," he told Beatrice the receptionist who let the phone ring fifteen times—he'd counted—while she poured everyone a cup of tea.

"Offset printing?" John the printer wrinkled his nose.

"An answering machine?" Beatrice didn't look as if she'd ever heard of one.

"Oh my, no." Percy spoke for them all. "We can't."

"Why not?"

Percy gave a simple shrug of his shoulders. "We've never done it that way before."

Famous last words.

"They're completely resistant to change," Gabe complained to Earl. "If it hasn't been done that way, it won't be done that way, *can't* be done that way!"

An answer phone, Beatrice had told him, would hurt people's feelings. "They'll think we don't want to speak to them."

"You think they don't get that idea when you don't answer the blasted phone now?"

"They know I'm busy. They'll ring back."

To do offset printing would offend the Fuge brothers, John the printer had said. The Fuge brothers came every Wednesday and helped with the typesetting. "They'll think they aren't needed," John told Gabe. "We wouldn't want that."

"Whose feelings would the computer hurt?" Gabe had asked.

"No one," Percy said. "But we haven't the electricity to handle it. Blow a fuse, we would. Shut everything down. Wouldn't want that now, would we?"

"It wouldn't take any more juice than an electric typewriter," Gabe argued, then realized that they were all staring at him. He looked around. There were no electric typewriters, only manuals.

"We're traditional here, you know," Percy said. "We've a history to uphold. The *Buckworthy Gazette* is An Institution. The journalistic equivalent of Stanton Abbey, if you will!"

Well, that Gabe could certainly agree with. There was a hell of a lot of rising damp in the employ of the *Buckworthy Gazette,* too.

What would Randall do?

He could, of course, ask. But he wasn't about to call Randall and admit ignorance.

"Well, things are going to change. I want all of you in my office for a meeting at three to discuss how we can turn this paper around."

They all stared. Then they began to shake their heads.

"Something wrong with three?" Gabe inquired with deadly calm.

"We always have tea at three," Beatrice said. Everyone nodded.

Gabe sucked in a breath. "Bring the pot. I'll have coffee. Black."

"We don't have coffee."

"Then that's the first thing we'll change."

The day went downhill from there.

They didn't have meetings on Tuesdays, Percy informed him.

"Well, we're having one today," Gabe said. "And if you don't want to come, I suggest you start cleaning out your desk."

There was a collective gasp.

Percy drew himself up to his full five feet seven. "You cannot threaten me, Mr. McBride. Nor can you fire me."

Gabe lifted a brow. "No?"

"No." Percy went into his own office where he opened a desk drawer and pulled out some papers. "It's a condition of the sale. It guarantees my employment."

Gabe skimmed them rapidly. It was there in black and white: if someone came to oversee the running of the *Gazette,* Percy Pomfret-Mumphrey was to be retained.

"Why the hell didn't you tell me I was getting Percy the Albatross hung around my neck?" he groused at Earl later.

"Ah, met Percy, have you?" Earl chuckled. "Well, I'm sure you can handle him. What did you say, two weeks and you'd have it all shaped up?"

"Two months," Gabe said through gritted teeth. He banged down the phone.

Save the *Buckworthy Gazette* in two months? Two millennia, more like!

He shut the door on them all and pored over recent editions of the *Gazette,* determined to get a feel for the newspaper. He had to start somewhere, and the end product seemed like the best place to figure out where things had gone wrong.

It was just like rebuilding a herd, actually. You looked at the beef and figured out why things weren't turning out the way you wanted them to. Then you set to work changing it. But you couldn't do that unless you knew your animals and the lay of the land.

At ten to five Beatrice told him there was a call for him. Earl? Again?

"What now?" he barked into the phone.

"Gabe? How's it going, then?" It was Randall, not Earl. A nervous, worried Randall, from the sound of him. "Are you all right?"

"Of course I'm all right! What do you think?" Gabe might have groused at Earl less than an hour before, but he damned well wasn't going to complain to Randall.

One word from him and his duty-driven cousin would be on the next plane home.

"I just…thought you might need a little moral support."

"Well, I don't. I'm fine. No problem," he lied through his teeth.

"Really?" Randall sounded dubious, but cautiously pleased.

"Nothing to worry about," Gabe said. "A child could do it." A child with access to explosives. "How are things at your end?"

"Fine," Randall said quickly and with excessive cheer. "Couldn't be better."

So Mr. Competent wasn't having any problems? Gabe felt oddly nettled. And more determined than ever to prove himself here. He rubbed a hand against the back of his neck. "Well, go find something to do. Cut wood. Feed the cattle. Sit in front of a roaring fire. Relax, damn it. And stop calling me up!"

"I was only checking," Randall said. "I'm…glad everything's going so well."

"It is," Gabe said firmly. "Don't call me again. Goodbye."

It was six o'clock, cold and damp and well past dark by the time he left the office. He made three trips to his car, lugging every piece of business correspondence he could find, all the ledgers and the last five years' worth of past papers to read. Then he got in and headed back toward the abbey.

He had no intention of going to the abbey, of course. He turned in at the dower house. It sat warm and welcoming on the hill, its windows cheerfully lit behind the trees. It was the one good thing in his life at the moment.

And in it was Freddie Crossman.

Freddie of the tumbling hair and the flowered nightgown. Freddie of the hip-hugging jeans and laughing eyes. He parked round the back, got out of the car and tapped on the kitchen door.

He could see her through the curtains behind the panes of glass. She didn't look surprised, just concerned as she opened the door. He turned on his best Montana cowboy grin. "Saw your sign. B&B. Full breakfast. Fifteen pounds. Sounds good to me."

Freddie's eyes got huge. She started to shut the door. "Oh,
but—"

"You're not full." He was positive about that.

"No, but—"

"I like rabbits," he assured her. He tried to look boyishly
charming. "And kids." He could see two now peeking from
around the corner of the dining room door. "And," he added
honestly, "I like you, Freddie Crossman."

"Oh, dear." Her hand went to her breast, as if it might
protect her.

Now that he'd seen her again—beautiful and bright and
tempting in spite of herself—Gabe could have told her: nothing would.

She let him in.

What else could she do?

Freddie had told herself all day long that she'd exaggerated
her awareness of him, that she'd been overwrought by the
elusive bunny yesterday and that was why the hairs on the
back of her neck had stood at attention, that was why his soft
Montana accent tantalized her, that was why she'd felt the
same sort of zing somewhere in the region of her heart that
she'd felt when she'd first met Mark. It wouldn't last, she'd
assured herself.

She was wrong.

Gabe McBride had every bit the same disastrous effect on
her equilibrium and good sense tonight that he'd had earlier.
She was a damn fool for opening her door to him.

But she had no choice.

She owed it to his grandfather. And even if she hadn't, how
could she tell her children, to whom she preached hospitality,
that she couldn't extend it here because Gabe McBride made
her hormones dance?

Charlie and Emma were avidly curious about their guest.

Freddie introduced them, then sent Charlie to get Gabe's
things out of his car, while she showed him to one of the guest
rooms in the converted attic. Emma followed, obviously entranced by this pied piper in cowboy boots and blue jeans.

"Why's he wearing those?" Freddie heard her whisper to Charlie when they came back down. She was looking at Gabe's boots.

"'Cause he's a cowboy," Charlie said.

Gabe must have overheard because he looked up at the boy and grinned. Charlie grinned back.

Freddie dished Gabe up a plate of the supper they'd just finished eating.

"Are you sure you've got enough?" he asked. "I can go down to the pub."

"There's plenty." She motioned for him to take a seat. Both children came and stood, watching him eat. She tried, with jerks of her head and shooing movements with her hands, to get them to leave. They didn't budge.

"Are you really a cowboy?" Emma asked. From the slightly worried look on her face, Freddie knew she was remembering Mrs. Peek proclaim a pair of renegade incompetent rob-you-blind plumbers as "cowboys" just last week.

"Not that kind of cowboy," Freddie hastened to explain.

"How many kinds are there?" Gabe lifted a curious brow. He was tucking into the shepherd's pie like he hadn't had a square meal in weeks.

"The television kind and the kind that screw things up," Charlie informed him.

Both brows shot up now.

"That's what a cowboy is...over here," Freddie explained.

"Not a compliment."

She shook her head. "No."

"We'll have to work on that. You know about real cowboys, don't you?" he asked Charlie.

Her son nodded emphatically. "Seen 'em on television. D'you shoot Indians?"

"No, I work with them."

"Can you yodel and play the guitar?" Emma asked.

Gabe laughed. "I can see I got here in the nick of time," he said to Freddie. "The *Gazette* is only half my job. I have to stay—to correct your children's misconceptions about cowboys."

* * *

The dower house beat the abbey by a mile. The rooms were warm, the meals were good, the bed was soft.

And even if he hadn't managed to share it with Freddie Crossman—*yet*—he still enjoyed the pleasure of her company.

Sort of. Actually he didn't get to spend much time with Freddie.

She was always busy when he was around—cooking, serving, cleaning, washing up. She barely sat still.

Good thing he liked to watch her move. He liked listening to her soft accent, too. It reminded him oddly—or maybe not so oddly—of home. His mother, after all, was British. Her accent was not that unlike Freddie's.

But that was the only way she reminded him of his mother. And the feelings she evoked in him had nothing to do with her maternal qualities at all.

She was, though, clearly a good mother. Charlie and Emma were polite and well-behaved, but not at all like little robots. They were eager and inquisitive, and they followed him around like young pups.

He liked Charlie and Emma enormously. He enjoyed listening to Charlie try to explain cricket to him, and was always eager to be "taste tester" when Emma helped her mother make scones or a cake. He loved telling them stories of cowboying and rodeoing. It was a kick to watch their eyes get big and their jaws hang open. He gloried in wrestling on the parlor floor with Charlie and delighted in getting down on his hands and knees and letting Emma have horse rides on his back while Charlie pretended he was much too old to want to do anything like that.

Partly he liked it because it was fun. But mostly he liked it because it was guaranteed to get a rise out of their mother.

"Charlie, don't pester," she would say.

"Emma, leave Mr. McBride alone now."

"They're fine. We're all fine," Gabe protested. "Come on in. Sit down." He patted the space on the sofa next to him. He knew she wanted to listen to his stories, too. He knew she was interested in them—in him.

Gabe McBride had been attracting women like honey did

bees since he was twelve years old. He recognized the signs—
even in a woman like Freddie who was determined not to
show it.

"How come you're stiff-arming me?" he asked her the
third night he was there. He and Charlie and Emma had become fast friends by then, but Freddie still kept her distance.
He'd done his best. He'd been funny and charming and he'd
played with her children. No hardship there. He liked them.
He'd taken them out to eat last night over Freddie's protests.
He'd gone to Emma's school program this afternoon because
Emma had invited him even though Freddie had tried to act
like he wasn't there.

Now he tracked her down after the children were in bed.
She was in the parlor, patching a pair of Charlie's trousers,
and she looked up warily. He came across the room and
dropped onto the sofa beside the chair where she sat.

"Stiff-arming?"

"Acting like a prig."

"Prig!" Freddie sputtered, her cheeks reddening.

Gabe grinned and stretched his arms over his head, easing
tired muscles. It never ceased to amaze him how much more
tired he got at a desk job than when he rode the range all day.
"See. You admit it."

"I never! I don't! I'm not a prig!"

"Then you're giving a damn good imitation of one. Loosen
up a little. Let go. You're beautiful when you smile."

She scowled at him, her cheeks reddening.

"See? Like that." He grinned and was rewarded by a twitch
at the corners of her mouth. "And let the kids play with me."

"I don't want them bothering you. You're a paying guest
and—"

"And in the interests of good hospitality, you shouldn't be
making me feel like one," Gabe said flatly. "You should be
making me feel at home."

"I'm trying, but—"

"Very trying," he agreed. "Come on. One more smile,"
he urged. "It won't kill you. I'll pay extra for it."

Freddie laughed reluctantly. And her laugh made the ex-

haustion of the day go away. It made Percy's pomposity and
Beatrice's worries and John's disapproving silence fade into
insignificance.

Gabe smiled, too. "That's better," he said softly. Then he
reached out a hand and, with one finger, touched hers.

She jerked hers away, of course.

"Okay," he said. "We'll stick with smiles. For now."

He didn't touch her again. He'd made the connection. That
was what mattered.

"You've taken a boarder, I hear." Mrs. Peek regarded Freddie over the top of her teacup.

It was four days since Gabe McBride had taken over their
lives, and Freddie was sure that the news had reached Mrs.
Peek within hours of the event. But the rain and sleet had been
relentless until now. This morning it was no more than a fine
drizzle. Mrs. Peek never let a fine drizzle slow her down.

Freddie concentrated on paring an apple for a pie. "He's
gone a great deal of the time. So it's really no bother."

"Of course it isn't," Mrs. Peek cackled. "Never a bother
having a han'sum fellow put his feet under your table. Better
yet in your bed." When Freddie spun around to protest, Mrs.
Peek said, "Time you married again, m'dear."

"I'm not interested in marrying again."

"Bah. Fine young gels need husbands. No sense pining
away. Us never pined."

When she wasn't having a fling with Lord Stanton, Mrs.
Peek had been marrying all and sundry. She'd been widowed
at least four times—the last as the result of the death of
Thomas Peek last winter.

"Seize your chances, m'dear. A good man doesn't turn up
on your doorstep everyday."

The "good man" being, of course, Gabe McBride.

Freddie supposed he was good. By some accounts anyway.
He was certainly working hard at the *Gazette*. And anyone
who drove Percy crazy—which the village grapevine assured
her he was doing—couldn't be all bad.

But more than he was a good man, he was a dangerous one. At least when it came to Freddie's peace of mind.

She hadn't got a good night's sleep since he'd arrived. She was too conscious of his footsteps above her head when she went to sleep at night, too aware of him whenever they sat across the table at mealtimes, and last night she'd almost jumped out of her skin when he'd deliberately reached out and touched her hand!

What did he think he was doing?

Don't be daft, Freddie, she admonished herself. It was clear what he was doing: he was coming on to her.

Flirting with her. Looking at her as if it was only a matter of time until there would be more between them than the fifteen pounds a night he was paying for his room.

She resisted even thinking in terms of "bed-and-breakfast" where Gabe McBride was concerned.

The "bed" part seemed far too intimate.

"Be good for the little tackers to have a man around, too," Mrs. Peek went on, unaware of the turmoil going on in Freddie's mind. "Likes 'em, I can tell."

And they adored him. The children were enthralled to have a real-live Montana cowboy living in their house. Once Emma had adjusted her definition of "cowboy," she'd been as enchanted as Charlie. Freddie tried to stop them bothering him, but he brushed off her concern.

He let Charlie clump around the house in his cowboy boots and wear his belt hitched tight enough so that it circled her son's narrow waist and proclaimed him the Salinas Champion Bull Rider.

To her dismay, he told both slack-jawed children exactly what a champion bull rider did. Last night she'd come upon all three of them, sitting on the bed in Charlie's room, long after both children should have been asleep.

"It's like ridin' a whirlwind," she heard him tell them. "Hangin' onto a hurricane. You know what a hurricane is, Em?"

As Freddie came to stand in the doorway, ready to lower the boom, she saw her daughter's eyes grow round and fill with excitement. "It's a storm," Emma said eagerly. "A big, big storm."

"Right. Well, you just imagine havin' that storm gathered right up underneath you. A ton of the meanest damn—er, darn—cow you've ever seen, just itchin' to run you through with one of his horns. An' he's lookin' at you, pawin' an' blowin', snortin' snot—"

"Bedtime," Freddie cut in.

"Not yet, Mum!" Charlie protested.

"We can't," Emma begged. "We have to hear what happened. Truly! Please, Gabe, tell us!"

"Mr. McBride," Freddie tried to correct.

Gabe raised his brows at her. "I told you. Friends use first names."

And Gabe and her children were obviously friends. While Freddie had been trying determinedly to steer clear of him, Charlie and Emma had been doing their best to get close.

They were, Freddie told herself, just starved for some masculine attention. But a *bull rider's*?

She could have wished for more discernment. A British "cowboy"—and all that that entailed—seemed almost preferable.

"It's nearly ten o'clock!"

"Please, Mum," Charlie's eyes were alight with an enthusiasm she'd begun to fear she would never see again. He had been six when Mark died—old enough to remember, to long for the adventures they had shared, to miss his father dreadfully.

"I'll make it short," Gabe promised. "You wouldn't want me to leave 'em hanging overnight, would you, Fred?"

And that was another thing! *Fred!*

He'd started calling her that the day after he arrived and had made the children giggle. Fred!

No one had ever dared call her Fred! Not even Mark—who was the most reckless person she'd ever known.

But Gabe did.

And now he just grinned at her, challenging her. His blue eyes were laughing, teasing her. It had been so long since anyone had teased her.

Freddie resisted the grin, she resisted the teasing in his eyes.

But she couldn't resist the story. She pressed her lips together. "All right. But make it quick."

"Eight seconds," Gabe promised solemnly. He patted the bed where he sat between Charlie and Emma. "Sit down, Fred. Get your daily dose of American culture."

"I have laundry to fold."

"You should hear, Mummy," Emma said. "It's scary!" She gave a little shiver and bounced next to Gabe, her expression gleeful.

"Eight seconds," Gabe promised again. "Frederica."

It was an olive branch. Of sorts.

Reluctantly Freddie sat.

It took longer than eight seconds. That was, apparently, how long a bull rider—the very words *bull rider* still made her shudder—had to stay on top of this bovine hurricane to make a qualified ride.

Qualified for what? Freddie wondered. The nuthouse?

In any case, it took five minutes at least for Gabe to embroider every one of those eight seconds, to describe every twist and turn, every dip and buck. His words permitted Freddie to envision every nasty moment from the instant the gate opened until he landed feet first in the dust and sprinted to climb over the fence while the bull tried to hook him from behind.

"But you made it. Didn't you?" Emma asked him breathlessly when he stopped.

"Course he did," Charlie said. "He's here, isn't he?"

Gabe put an arm around Emma's small shoulders. "I'm still here, sweetheart."

The gentle way he looked at her daughter made Freddie's heart squeeze tight. Or maybe it was hearing the endearment. *Sweetheart.* She hoped Emma didn't read too much into it.

Gabe was, after all, just passing through. He was here to sort out the *Gazette,* that was all. He had a life back in Montana. He wasn't going to stay.

Freddie stood abruptly. "Very nice. Very well told. Excellent story," she said briskly. "Come along now," she said to the children.

"But—" Charlie began, ready to angle for another tale.

Gabe stood up, too. "You heard your mother. Time to hit the hay."

The phrase made Emma giggle. "Like a cow?"

Gabe ruffled her hair. "Like a cowboy. Or a cowgirl."

"Are there cowgirls?" Emma's eyes were big again.

"You bet. There's one back home—" He smiled as if he was remembering someone special "—called Claire."

His girlfriend? Freddie wondered. Was Claire eagerly waiting for Gabe to come back? Probably. She imagined American women were equally susceptible to his charm, even if they didn't find him as exotic as she did.

Emma didn't care about those things. "Can I be a cowgirl?"

Gabe nodded. "You go hit the hay now, and you've got a good start."

Emma allowed herself to be herded toward her bedroom, but she hung onto his hand, talking as they went. "What else do cowgirls do?"

"Everything cowboys do," Gabe replied with a grin. "Only they think they do it better."

Emma giggled. "Will you teach me?"

"Emma!" Freddie protested. "Mr. McBride—Gabe—has work to do. It's been very kind of him just to tell you stories."

"He could show me other stuff," Emma said stubbornly.

"Like roping." Charlie followed them out of his bedroom. "I'd like to know how to rope. And brand. And—"

"No branding," Gabe said, "But I'll teach you to rope."

"We don't have a rope!" Freddie felt like the little boy with his thumb in the dike.

Gabe didn't even seem to hear. "And maybe we could find a horse or two and go riding."

"Enough!" Freddie raised her voice. "Bedtime." She glared at him. "Eight seconds. You promised."

He opened his mouth. Their eyes met. He closed his mouth. He nodded, then looked sternly from one child to the other.

"Hit the hay now," he said gently. "Both of you. Cowboys—and cowgirls—do what the boss tells 'em to."

Unfortunately there were no cowboys or cowgirls working for the *Gazette*.

So Gabe did it all. He called the local electrician to update the wiring. He ordered three computers and all the relevant software. He bought coffee.

And then he waited expectantly, as no doubt Randall would have done, for the *Gazette* employees to see which way their leader had pointed and hop to and get things done.

After a week-and-a-half, the lights were brighter. There were power points—the British not only didn't understand him when he talked, they had different words for everything, even electrical outlets!—galore, but the computers sat on the desks unbooted and the software still hadn't been opened.

Neither had the coffee.

The editorials were as pompous and as unrelated to village concerns as they'd ever been. And there were no new local advertisers even though he'd told Beatrice to call every shop in town.

Gabe was ready to tear his hair. So much for the voice of authority. So much for being lord and master.

It might work for Randall, but it damn sure didn't work for him.

Of course Randall's reputation for hard work and smart decisions preceded him. They knew they could trust him.

Gabe had no reputation. He was, he realized as he sat behind his desk, like a new foreman, untried, untested. Untrusted.

And just like that new straw boss, he'd have to prove himself. That was the problem here. He'd been trying to be Randall when he should have been himself.

He stood up. He flung everything he could find into his briefcase—God, a briefcase! What had he become?—and announced that he was going home.

"Home?" Beatrice looked up, startled. "To America?"

Percy was triumphant. "So much for cowboy ways," he muttered as Gabe headed toward the door.

Gabe stopped and turned back. "I'm going to Mrs. Crossman's to map out our route. I'll be here on Monday bright and early," he said, his gaze moving from one mystified face to the next and finally settling on Percy. A slow smile spread across Gabe's. "Get ready to cowboy up."

Three

There was supposed to be a ghost at Stanton Abbey. A Presence, with a capital *P*. A monk fretting about how he and his brethren were tossed out on their ears by Henry VIII. Freddie had never met him. She wasn't inclined to believe in the presence of something not there.

Until Gabe McBride moved into her house.

Then, even when he wasn't there physically—even when she knew he was well and truly out of the house, down at the *Gazette* or over at the pub—somehow he was still there.

Of course he was, she thought irritably. Charlie and Emma never stopped talking about him. They lived and breathed Gabe McBride.

"Gabe can do this...Gabe thinks that...Do you think Gabe would like to...Gabe's teaching me to rope...Gabe's teaching me to ride...God bless Mummy and Granny and Gran'pa and Gabe."

Was it any wonder, Freddie thought, that she couldn't get him out of her mind?

She blamed Charlie and Emma and Gabe himself, but she knew the fault was at least partly hers. There was some fatal flaw deep inside her that worked like a magnet, drawing her toward unsuitable men.

It might have helped if she'd been able to go out to work everyday. She could have distracted herself.

But as caretaker, she spent the day on the grounds and in the abbey where every time she turned around generations of Stantons, many of whom had the same dark hair and deep blue eyes as Gabe McBride, stared down at her. It was like being surrounded with two-dimensional versions of a man already inhabiting her head.

And then at night she went home to the real thing.

He was becoming like a member of the family, just as he preferred. The children were thrilled. Freddie was not. He was too handsome, too active, too…too…*male.*

He made her want things she knew she shouldn't want.

He made the kids want things they shouldn't want either—like adventure, excitement, danger. Risks.

"A little adventure never hurt anyone," Gabe said. "They're entirely too sheltered. They need a little excitement."

Storytelling, Freddie thought. That was excitement enough. Gabe and the children disagreed.

When Freddie woke up Saturday morning, the house was extraordinarily quiet.

For a few minutes she thought that they'd all had a long lie-in. Then she realized that, while Gabe was grown up enough to appreciate the value of a late weekend morning, Charlie and Emma would *never* waste a Saturday morning on sleep!

Something was seriously amiss.

Freddie bolted out of bed, grabbed her dressing gown and ran to check the bedrooms. As she'd feared, both children were gone. She clattered down the stairs. Cereal bowls were rinsed and stacked on the counter. The table was wiped clean—except for a note.

"We've gone to be cowboys," Charlie had written, "in Bolts' field."

Cowboys? In Bolts' field?

Josiah Bolt raised sheep! No, surely not.

But half an hour later when she finally reached the stone wall bounding Bolts' field, Gabe was showing Charlie how to lay a lasso over the head of a very bewildered sheep.

"You don't rope sheep!" Freddie exclaimed, clambering over the stile.

Gabe just looked up and grinned at her. "I do."

"Josiah will go round the bend! He's not the easiest neighbor to get along with in the first place," Freddie railed. "I know him! He'll say you're endangering the quality of the wool!"

Gabe broke out laughing.

"Trust me. He will," Freddie said. "And it can't be good for the sheep in any case. I mean, they're not meant to be roped. And Stantons have always been in the forefront of agricultural responsibility. Quite looked up to, they are, and—"

Gabe shoved his hat back on his head. "You made your point. We won't rope."

Both children looked at him, crestfallen, then at Freddie, accusing.

"We won't rope *sheep*," Gabe amended. "We'll find us something else to rope," he promised the children. "Maybe we can borrow a cow." He looked at Freddie. "Who keeps cows?"

"Well, the earl, of course. He has prize Herefords."

"Not them," Gabe said. "Earl'd have my hide. We need a retired cow."

Within hours he had Stella.

Stella. She was big and brown and mud-caked and Mrs. Peek, who just happened to drop by, knew that Mr. Ware was selling her because her milk production was down.

"He don't want to. 'Er's a member of the family, like," Mrs. Peek said. "But he's a businessman for all that. And you know 'er'll be for the knacker's yard if he don't sell 'er."

"The knacker?" Charlie and Emma were horrified.

"We'll have her," Gabe said.

Mr. Ware delivered her to the dower house that afternoon. Gabe put her in the small barn.

"We don't keep cows," Freddie objected.

"Now you do."

And apparently she did. The children were overjoyed. Gabe seemed as if a weight had been lifted from his shoulders. He was whistling as he brought Stella a barrow full of hay.

"Making her comfortable," Freddie said sardonically.

"Hey, you're the one who was carrying on about agricultural responsibility."

"So I was." She watched as Gabe forked the hay into the stall. "Who's going to milk her?"

He blinked. Then something that might have been a flush peeked above the collar of his jacket. He scratched his ear. He chewed his lip. He looked around a little desperately.

"You're a cowboy," Freddie reminded him.

"I've never milked a cow."

"Never?" She was amazed.

"Cowboys don't!"

Freddie smiled. "They do now."

She had to give Gabe credit.

He was obviously not keen on milking cows, but when she said, "If you can teach Charlie and Emma to rope, I guess I can teach you to milk a cow," he cocked his head and looked at her, a small smile playing around his mouth.

"Guess so. If you'll show me how."

Freddie, who hadn't milked a cow since she was twelve years old and spending the summer holidays at her grandparents' small farm in Somerset, said blithely, "Of course."

It would serve him right for her to be the one in control for a change.

Moments later, seated at Stella's side with Gabe crouched next to her, his fingers beneath hers as she attempted to show him the right way to pull the teat, she had serious second thoughts.

She'd never thought of milking a cow as foreplay. Suddenly she did.

She tried to tell herself it was ridiculous, that Gabe certainly wasn't thinking sexual thoughts while they were thus engaged.

But there was something excruciatingly intimate about their proximity, about what they were doing.

Their hands were touching. So were their thighs. His head was so close her hair brushed his cheek—and his brushed hers. She could hear the soft intake of his breath, could feel it on her lips when he turned his head to grin at her as the first stream of milk from the cow's teat hit the bucket.

His mouth was that close...and moving closer.

"Never mind!" She practically leaped to her feet, knocking him sideways and almost tipping over the tin pail. "You're right. Cowboys don't milk cows. I'll do it myself!"

He laughed up at her from where he sat on the straw. "You sure, Fred?"

Her cheeks were burning. "Yes, Gabriel," she drawled. "I'm sure."

The Gabriel bit was supposed to put him in his place. To annoy him the way being called "Fred" annoyed her.

But he just grinned. "My mother named me after the angel."

"Your mother named you after seven other Stantons," Freddie retorted. "I see them hanging in the abbey every single day. Glowering down at me."

Gabe's grin widened. "And you think of me."

"I do not!"

"Liar." His voice was soft and teasing and set all the hairs on the back of her neck to standing at attention.

She couldn't argue because Charlie and Emma suddenly barreled into the barn.

"Is she milked? Can we start ropin' now?" Charlie asked.

"Not yet," Gabe said. "She needs a little cooling off time."

His gaze met Freddie's. She blushed. Then she picked up the pail and started toward the house. "I'm going to fix dinner," she said, trying to sound casual and indifferent. "You three can play cowboy for another hour."

"Not without Stella," Charlie said glumly.

"There's nothing to do if we can't rope Stella," Emma added.

"Take Mr....take Gabe up to the abbey," Freddie suggested. "Maybe you can rope the ghost."

They often took B&B guests to the abbey. Regaling visitors with the tale of the Stanton Abbey ghost was always good fun. And whom better to tell than the man whose ancestors had usurped the ghost's home?

"What ghost? What are you talking about?" Gabe looked both wary and baffled, as if afraid Freddie was having him on.

"Didn't you ever hear about the ghost?" she asked.

"Randall used to make up stories about one," Gabe said. "I never believed him."

"Perhaps you should have," she said with a twinkle in her eye. "Charlie will tell you all about it," she promised.

Charlie needed no further urging. "It's a monk," she heard him telling Gabe. "Almost seven feet tall and carrying his head under his arm—"

"Charlie!" she admonished.

"Sorry." He grinned at Gabe. "He's still got his head. But he goes howling through the abbey on moonless nights, 'cause he's unhappy that Henry VIII threw out the monks and..."

They wandered out of earshot, off in the direction of the abbey, and Freddie breathed a sigh of relief.

"He might have kissed me," she told Stella, still trembling just slightly from her narrow escape.

Stella, her mouth full of unchewed hay, looked back with bovine indifference.

Dinner was ready and the table was set. The door banged open, and Gabe and the children stamped into the kitchen.

"We're gonna stay at the abbey!" Charlie yelled.

"An' see the ghost!" Emma shouted.

"An' write a story about it," Charlie went on.

"Tonight," Emma finished.

Freddie stared at them—then at the man standing behind them. "I beg your pardon?"

"We're going to spend the night in the abbey," Gabe said. "Check out this seven-foot tall headless monk. Write him up for posterity—in the *Gazette*."

That was what Freddie thought she'd heard.

"I really don't think…" she began, then her voice faded as she realized all three of them were holding their breath. Charlie's and Emma's looks beseeched her.

"We won't be scared, Mum," Charlie said stoutly. "Promise."

"Course not," Emma added, then chewed on her lip. Freddie saw her daughter's fingers edge out to grip Gabe's strong thigh. His hand slid down to cover Emma's smaller one.

"Charlie's always wanted to," Gabe said. "He said you promised he could when he found an adult willing to do it." His clear blue eyes challenged her. "I'm adult," he told her quite unnecessarily. "And I'm willing."

Freddie swallowed. Her fingers knotted.

"If you're worried, come along."

"Come along? You mean, spend the night…" Again her voice faded, this time from breathlessness.

Gabe nodded. "Spend the night," he affirmed. "With me." He winked at her.

Heat crawled up Freddie's neck and face.

"And us, too," Emma put in, blissfully unaware of the adult subtext.

"She knows we're going to be there," Charlie said scornfully. "What do you say, Mum? Will you come?"

All three of the looked at her again, breath bated, eyes sparkling—the children's with enthusiasm, Gabe's with something…something else.

She shouldn't.

But she had, in fact, told Charlie he could do it in the company of a willing adult. And now, heaven help her, he had one.

And Emma wanted to go, too. She could hardly expect Gabe

McBride to deal with both of them. They were her children, after all.

It was only for one night. The abbey was huge. There was nothing to say they had to be, all of them, in one room.

"All right," she said at last, to the sound of an incredible exhalation of pent-up apprehension. "Yes."

If Earl could see them now, Gabe thought with a hint of a grin as he folded his arms behind his head and looked around the dimly lit master bedroom of Stanton Abbey.

There they were, all four of them, piled—amid sleeping bags, flashlights, empty cups of Horlicks and the remains of two packets of chocolate biscuits—in the ancient sumptuous bed that had held generations of lordly Stantons for the past umpteen hundred years.

Earl would have a fit.

Freddie had had a fit on his behalf.

"We can't stay there!" she'd protested when Gabe had led them into the bedroom.

"You said this is where he appears."

"I know, but—"

"So how can we see him if we're not there?" And ignoring her protests, he'd herded them all in and begun to spread sleeping bags on the bed.

"We're really going to stay here?" Charlie's eyes had gone wide and round at the sight of the huge high bed with its heavy brocade curtains and canopy.

"All n-night?" Emma wanted to know. She'd looked nervously from Gabe to her mother, swallowing hard.

"Not—" Freddie began.

"—all night," Gabe finished. "Only until we see the ghost. Unless—" he grinned at the children "—you fall asleep."

They'd stared at him, astonished. As if! they seemed to say.

Now it was barely midnight, and both of them were already zonked.

Of course it had taken a lot of energy to jump at every creak and rattle, to shiver at the sound of an owl overhead, to gasp, "What was that?" at the drafts that blew in around the window frames and moved like a spiritual presence through the room.

No wonder they were tired.

As close as they'd come to seeing the Stanton Abbey ghost was a mouse that had scuttled from one side of the room to the other. Emma's shrieks had scared the mouse almost as much as it had scared them.

After that, and after Freddie's exhortations to settle down, they'd subsided into watchfulness. They'd watched for the ghost. Freddie had watched them.

Gabe had watched Freddie.

In the dim light he could barely make her out, but it didn't stop him trying.

It had been a stroke of genius getting them all in here together so he had the leisure to look his fill. During the day he was gone. At meal times she was flitting about and the children were clamoring for his attention.

But tonight, once the chatter had died down and the children had settled, Gabe had had the opportunity at last to simply look at Freddie Crossman.

He'd have liked to do a lot more than look.

It didn't seem to matter how much he berated himself for this obsession with a totally unsuitable woman—an English-woman! a widow! the mother of children!—he'd stopped telling himself she was too old for him, but everything else still applied—he couldn't quell the attraction he felt.

It's because there's no one else, he told himself every day.

But in fact that wasn't true.

Just yesterday he'd met two of Buckworthy's beauties in the street outside the *Gazette.* Their grandmother had introduced herself—and them—to him.

"Aurora Ponsonby," she told him, "an old friend of his lordship."

It took a minute for Gabe to realize she was talking about Earl. Then he'd done his best to be polite and make small talk with them, though he'd have much preferred to be making mincemeat out of Percy because Percy had followed him out to deliver a long-winded spiel about something else that had never been done before.

He'd barely noticed the Ponsonby females. It hadn't occurred to him until later that there was calculation in the introduction, that Aurora Ponsonby had been extolling her granddaughters' virtues rather heavy-handedly. Did she consider him a catch, then?

Didn't matter. He wasn't interested in being caught.

But he *was* interested in Freddie.

He wondered how smart this had actually been, getting them on the bed together, when absolutely nothing could happen.

Well, maybe not absolutely nothing...

He flexed his shoulders against the headboard of the bed and eased himself closer to her.

"They're asleep. We can go," Freddie whispered.

"Hmm?"

"You said—"

"We'd wake them up when we go. We're not going yet."

"We can't stay here all night!"

"Why not?"

"Because," she began. Then abruptly stopped. She looked at him quickly in the dimness, then just as quickly, she looked away. "We have to go," she muttered, but she sounded like she was trying to convince herself as much as him.

"Just a little longer." He grinned faintly. "Who knows? The ghost might really show up."

"You don't believe that now any more than you did when you were ten."

"Oh, I'm a lot different than I was when I was ten," he told her, his voice rough with a desire his ten-year-old self had had no inkling of.

Freddie plucked at the sleeping bag that was tucked around her and Emma. Then she let out a soft sigh and settled back once more. He breathed a little easier.

"You've worked really hard on the abbey," he said after a few minutes. Even though it still seemed like the dampest, coldest place on earth to him, the guided tour she had taken

him on earlier in the evening taught him just how much upkeep was required and how well she'd done.

"I try," she said. "I'm not sure I'm the best person for the
job, but Lord Stanton insisted..."

"How long have you been doing it?"

"Since my husband died. Mark worked for the earl. He died
in a storm bringing the yacht back from Calais, and for some
reason his lordship felt responsible. He shouldn't have," she
said earnestly. "It was Mark who was reckless. Mark who
took the risk. No one asked him to!" She stopped abruptly,
apparently aware that any further exclamations might wake the
children.

"Do you..." He stopped, unsure how to ask, still, for rea-
sons he didn't want to examine too closely, needing to. "Do
you still miss him?" Now there was a stupid question! She'd
loved him, married him. Of course she missed him! "A lot, I
mean?"

For a minute Gabe didn't think she was going to answer,
and he knew the question was as impertinent as it had been
awkward. "I'm sorry. I had no right. I—"

"I miss him," Freddie answered. "But it's kind of a hollow
feeling now. An emptiness. Not pain anymore. Sometimes, I
just get angry. I think, 'what a waste.' He's missing his children! He's not going to see them grow up." Her fingers knotted on the sleeping bag again.

And Gabe, before he could stop himself, reached out and
wrapped his hand around hers. He thought she might pull
away so he tightened his grip just a little.

But after a split second's resistance, Freddie's hand relaxed
in his. Slowly Gabe let his breath out, rubbed his thumb
against her knuckle. Curved his fingers around hers. Didn't
move. Just sat. Breathed.

Desired.

Wanted.

Freddie Crossman.

A lot.

A whole lot.

He ran his tongue over suddenly parched lips. He shifted,

trying to get a little more room inside his jeans. His thumb moved to caress the side of her hand. Her skin was so soft. He knew she worked hard, but her fingers still seemed softer than any he'd ever touched. He brought them to his lips.

Freddie sucked in a sharp breath. Gabe felt a faint tremor in her hand. He sensed one running through her whole body. But she didn't pull away as he pressed his mouth lightly against her fingers.

"G-Gabe?" There was only a hint of protest in her voice. It was breathless, and she sounded as hungry as he was.

"Mmm." He didn't move his mouth, just murmured against her hand, let his tongue slide out from between his lips and touched it to her fingers.

"Gabe!" Shock, but no less hunger.

"Fred." Hell of a thing to be whispering! It almost made him laugh. His lips curved and he nibbled her fingers, then he eased himself around the sleeping Emma and took her mother into his arms.

She came willingly, all the time saying softly, "We can't do this!"

"Sure we can."

"The children—"

"Are out like lights, both of them."

"We can't— We're not—" She stiffened.

"We won't," Gabe promised, soothing. "Just kissing, Fred. Just…touching."

"P-promise?"

He promised—and meant it.

He didn't need an audience for what he wanted to do with Freddie Crossman. He didn't want their first time to be furtive and groping and quick. He wanted to take his time, to love her fully. And he was no callow boy. He might want her desperately, but he could wait.

In the meantime, though, he could heighten the pleasure for both of them. He could kiss and stroke and nibble and touch. So he did.

He moved slowly, taking his time, relishing the experience. And after a few moments of tension where Freddie barely seemed to breathe, finally, slowly, she began to relax in his embrace. Her lips touched his cheek, nuzzled his neck, sent a shiver of longing right down to his core.

Gabe bit his lip. *You promised,* he reminded himself. *You're tough. In control.*

Oh, yeah.

"M-maybe this wasn't such a great idea," he whispered hoarsely, pulling back, edging away.

She blinked, looked at him, worried. "N-no?" She sounded crestfallen.

"I want—" But he couldn't blurt out what he wanted. She knew. He bent his head and sucked in a harsh breath. "I want it to be right."

He lifted his gaze to see if she understood. He wasn't even sure he understood exactly what he meant by that. He just knew this wasn't it.

She looked confused, then her expression cleared. A small smile touched her lips. "Oh, Gabe," she whispered. And then she leaned toward him and touched her lips to his; her tongue touched his.

So much for control.

"Fred!" He jerked back, gasping.

"Huh? D'ja see 'im?" Charlie's eyes blinked open.

Freddie yanked herself upright against the headboard. Gabe, aching, gritted his teeth and tried to answer. "Just heard a noise. Pounding sound."

The blood in his veins. Throbbing. Pulsing. Beating him to death.

Charlie rubbed his eyes and yawned. "Stupid ghost," he muttered. He scooted up the bed and laid his head in his mother's lap. His eyes shut. He slept.

Over the children Gabe and Freddie looked at each other. She smiled a little wryly.

"Maybe we should just go home," he said.

Freddie sang as she folded the laundry. She did clever little dance steps while she dusted the parlor. She hummed as she cooked dinner.

"Glad to see you're smiling more," Mrs. Peek had said just this morning when she'd stopped by.

"What?" Freddie hadn't been aware of any such thing.

"Of course, that han'sum Gabe McBride'd make any woman smile."

"I don't know what you mean," Freddie lied.

But Mrs. Peek just smiled. She was in love with Gabe herself, and not just because he was "han'sum." Because on Monday when she'd come by as Gabe was leaving for the office, he asked her to come work for him.

For the first time in her life, Mrs. Peek had been speechless. She'd stared at him with round, astonished eyes. "You want us to work for 'ee, Mr. McBride?"

"You bet I do. You understand this community a whole lot better than plummy Percy." And he'd put her bicycle in the back of the Range Rover and the two of them had gone off to the *Gazette* together.

Later he told Freddie he reckoned Mrs. Peek was a woman to ride the river with.

"What?" Freddie looked at him, mystified.

"It's what we say about a good hand. You can trust him with your life. Mrs. Peek's like that. Besides, she's a natural for the staff. She has a finger in every pie—and an ear in every house. She's without a doubt the best news gatherer in the county. Stantons might as well pay her for doing what she's going to do anyway."

Best of all, Percy had had a fit about it.

It was the beginning of the end for Percy.

Mrs. Peek gathered news. Gabe wrote it.

"I'll do the editorial this week," he told Percy the day he hired Mrs. Peek.

"But we've never—"

"You bet we haven't," Gabe cut in, "but we're starting to. Now."

And when Percy had continued to bluster, Gabe had said, "You know how we settle these things in Montana?" He'd curled his fingers into fists.

Percy mumbled, shuffled, and, according to Gabe, "hightailed it out of the office just like that. He didn't seem to want to slug it out," Gabe said. He was wearing a wide, satisfied grin.

Things continued to improve at the *Gazette*.

Gabe commandeered Beatrice. He made his own coffee, bought a box of tea bags for everyone else and told her she was now in charge of advertising.

"Me?" Beatrice stared at him.

"Why not you? You know everyone in Buckworthy." He took her door to door in Buckworthy, introducing himself and Beatrice to each and every shopkeeper.

"They all know me," Beatrice protested.

"That's the point. They know you, not me. You're going to help us connect. You're going to help the *Gazette* figure out how to help them."

So with Beatrice at his side, Gabe went around the entire village, shook every hand and sat down to discuss the *Gazette*. He asked each one how to make the paper best serve the town and the surrounding villages. It was the first time in memory anyone had asked. The shopkeepers talked to him. They talked to Beatrice. And, as always, they talked to Mrs. Peek.

"We need a lot more Mrs. Peeks," he told Freddie. "One or two per village."

"Try the Women's Institute." She could just imagine what they'd say when a booted, jeans-clad Montana cowboy showed up among those sedate, virtuous ladies. Gabe McBride would really give them something to pray about.

She thought he wouldn't go. But she learned very quickly not to underestimate Gabe McBride.

"Great idea," he told her afterward. "It helped that they'd read my editorial in today's paper. They seemed to know who I was."

Freddie could have told him they'd known who he was the minute he set foot in the county. But she couldn't have predicted his success—on his own terms.

"He's a breath of fresh air," Mrs. Peek said.

Freddie thought, a whirlwind more like.

Certainly he'd swept through her life and turned it upside

down. He'd made her heart beat faster, her pulse race. He'd made her feel alive again.

She was exhilarated. And scared.

She shouldn't be humming and dancing and singing, and she knew it.

There was no future for her and Gabe McBride.

He'd made no secret that he wasn't stopping. He was going home to Montana in weeks, days even. He'd made no bones about being single and determined to stay that way.

She wondered about this Claire he'd mentioned, but a few circumspect questions convinced her that he wasn't interested in Claire—or any other woman. He was playing the field.

And yet...

And yet the night they'd spent together in the bed at the abbey, he hadn't pressed. Of course he wouldn't. How could he with Emma and Charlie there. But he'd kissed. His eyes had promised. And he'd said, "I want it to be right."

As if sometime it would be.

Freddie wanted it, too. Desperately. She wanted Gabe.

She was a fool.

She couldn't help it.

Four

Percy didn't give in easily.

Gabe didn't care. And not only because he relished a good fight.

Once he figured out that the same determination that went into riding a bull and working cattle would help him with the *Gazette,* once he understood that he didn't have to be Randall to succeed, life got a whole lot easier.

And if Percy wanted to draw himself up to his full five feet seven and say, ''Over my dead body,'' every day, well, that was fine with Gabe.

It would give him that much more time to stay with Freddie and the kids.

It amazed him how involved he'd become with Freddie and her family in a few short weeks. The sheep roping led to the cow roping. Nightly stories of life in the west led to him tracking down videos of movies about cowboys and about rodeo. Charlie and Emma had never seen a bull ride. So he called Randall and made him overnight them a video of the National Finals.

He'd made up his mind to refuse to discuss the *Gazette,* but Randall hadn't even asked. Gabe forgot to ask about the ranch.

He got the video converted to the proper format and showed it to the children with rousing success. He loved watching Charlie and Emma, their jaws dropping at the sight of the spinning, twisting, bucking bull—and the cowboy trying to make his eight-second ride.

And that led them to wanting to do some riding of their own.

"Absolutely not!" Freddie said. "You are not teaching my children to ride a bull!"

"Horses, Fred. Broke ones. They can't be cowboys—or girls—if they can't ride." And, taking Freddie's reluctant silence as approval, he went looking for some horses to borrow. Mrs. Peek, bless her heart, knew exactly who to contact. And the next day he had horses for all of them.

Even Freddie.

At first she protested. Then he reminded her that they were *her* children. Didn't she want to supervise what they were learning? Didn't she want to witness their triumphs? Be there when they succeeded?

So she came. And she rode. In fact she was a good rider.

He was the one who fell off!

It was downright embarrassing. And it wasn't even his fault. It was the damned pheasant—and the skittish horse—and most especially that ridiculous little English saddle. There was no place to get a grip!

"Are you all right?" Freddie and the children bent over him worriedly.

His pride was hurt. And his rear end.

Gabe scrambled up. "I'm fine," he muttered, swatting at the mud that caked the back of his jeans.

"Yoo-hoo!" In the distance, at the edge of the road, he spied Mrs. Peek, red sweater flapping, as she waved from where she'd parked her bicycle. She whipped out a little notebook and began to scribble.

Gabe groaned.

Freddie laughed, delighted. "I wonder what the headline will read."

"Editor axes new local writer," Gabe grumbled. "Literally."

But Freddie, still laughing, just shook her head. "She's taking her job seriously."

Gabe laughed ruefully, too, acknowledging the old lady's dedication. She was thrilled to be published. Her first column of local news had come out last Thursday "over Percy's dead body," and she'd been walking on air since.

Everywhere Gabe looked now, he saw a red-sweatered Mrs. Peek, pedaling her bicycle furiously in pursuit of more local coverage, hoping to scoop Mrs. Bolt and Mrs. Nute from the Women's Institute.

He could only hope that his getting thrown came during an otherwise heavy news week.

He seemed happy here.

Freddie watched him play with the children, teach them to rope and to ride. She watched him cheer Mrs. Peek on and exult with every triumph that brought the moribund *Gazette* further from the brink of extinction. She watched him sprawl easily in the parlor and look at her from beneath hooded eyes, making it obvious that he was looking for "the right time."

And even though she knew she shouldn't, she couldn't help thinking things she had no business thinking—about what it would be like to love—and be loved by—Gabe McBride.

He would leave.

Of course he would leave. There was never any doubt. He talked about the ranch constantly to the children.

"Back home..." he would say. "On the ranch..."

It sounded wonderful—a land so vast and empty with its high snow-capped mountains and broad valleys that she could scarcely imagine it.

So he called Randall again and asked him to send pictures of the ranch, of the family, of his rodeo career.

The children were spellbound. So was Freddie.

"Wow," Charlie breathed. "It's awesome."

"Is that the bunkhouse?" Emma wanted to know as they sat in the parlor, the pictures spread out all across the table. Gabe held her on his knee. Charlie stood next to him, pushing the photos around, looking at first one and then the next, then going back, as if he couldn't take it all in.

"That's a *lot* of cows," Emma said, pointing at one of a round-up.

"An' a lot of cowboys," Charlie said, awestruck. "I wish I could be a cowboy."

Gabe ruffled his hair. "Maybe you will be someday."

Freddie, seeing the hero-worship in her son's face, bit her lip to keep from saying sharply, "Don't hold out false hopes."

There was such a light in Charlie's eyes these days, such a bounce to his step, she couldn't bring herself to say anything. He hadn't been this bright-eyed and eager since before Mark's death. And even though she knew she shouldn't encourage him to pursue this cowboy business, she still couldn't deflate his hopes.

Not now. Not yet.

After all, Charlie knew how unlikely it was. He wasn't a baby anymore.

He knew that Gabe would leave. Gabe had never made it a secret that his time in Buckworthy was limited. So Charlie couldn't be crushed when it actually happened.

And he would always have the memories later on.

That's what Freddie told herself anyway. She hoped it would be enough.

And not just for Charlie.

"That's enough for tonight," she said briskly after they'd spent most of another evening poring over the pictures. "It's past bedtime."

"But we've got all the rodeo pictures to look at!" Charlie protested.

"Please, Mummy," Emma beseeched. "I wanta see Gabe ridin' a bull!"

"You've seen Gabe ride a bull on the video." She had, too. Until she'd closed her eyes in stark terror.

"But—"

Gabe pushed back his chair and set Emma on her feet. "Real cowboys follow orders. Move it."

And they did. All it took was one word from Gabe and they scampered off.

"They were going to do what I told them to," Freddie muttered.

"I know." Gabe smiled at her. "I just wanted to hurry 'em along a little." The way he was looking at her, smiling at her, sent a shiver of awareness up her spine.

"Why?" she asked warily.

"Because of this." And he reached out, drew her gently into his arms and kissed her.

It was a hungry kiss, a deep kiss, a kiss that told Freddie that Gabe had been thinking about it for a good long time—probably as long as she had. And it felt so warm, so wonderful, so right, that she was returning it before she had a chance to think.

It had been so long. She had been so lonely.

She hadn't realized until Gabe arrived how lonely her life had become. There were the children, of course. They loved her, and she them. They challenged her, and she tried to keep up with them.

But until Gabe there had been no man. No one to meet Freddie face-to-face, toe-to-toe, one-to-one.

She'd thought she didn't care, had believed she hadn't had time to miss it.

She was wrong.

The touch of him, the heat of him, the strength of him—all of it—told her she'd been very, very wrong.

And when he sat back down and took her with him, brought her down on his lap and still never stopped kissing her, she went right with him, as hungry as he was, as desperate as he was.

His fingers tugged her shirttails from her trousers. His hands slid up beneath, caressing her heated skin. She murmured against his lips, felt his tongue press for entrance, and opened up for him. Against her bottom she could feel the press of his need for her, hard and insistent. She shifted, turning in his arms, rubbing against him through wool and denim.

He groaned.

"Mummy! I left my—oh!" It was Emma. Halfway down

the stairs, eyes popping out of her head, face as red as a beet—
as red as her mother's face.

Freddie leapt out of Gabe's arms, shoving away so hard she
almost knocked his chair over. With one hand she tried to
smooth her hair. With the other she stabbed ineffectually at
her shirttails, trying to tuck them back in.

"You what, Em?" she croaked. Oh, heavens, her voice
didn't even work!

"L-left my m-maths book down here." Still Emma hesitated on the steps, tipping from one foot to the other, her eyes
going from her mother to Gabe and back again. She looked
as if she might burst.

"Come get it then. Put it in your book bag or you'll forget
it in the morning." Freddie gave up on the shirt. She tried to
sound brisk and set about scraping the photos into a pile, as
if she had been cleaning and the heightened color in her face
was merely from exertion. She couldn't look at Gabe.

Emma did. She studied both of them as she came slowly
down the steps, and Freddie knew she wasn't fooled. Her eyes
sparkled. She pressed her lips together to keep from smiling
as she got the book from the sideboard and, with one last look,
scurried back upstairs again.

"Charlie!" Freddie heard her whisper loudly. "Guess
what!"

It was Freddie's turn to groan.

Gabe laughed.

"It isn't funny!" she said, stricken.

"Well, not in some respects," he agreed, adjusting his jeans
carefully and wincing as he did so. "But, hey, it happens."

"Well, it won't happen again." She didn't look at him. She
moved quickly, putting the photos into the folders Lord Stanton had sent them in. Then she stacked them in neat piles. Her
hands shook.

Gabe came up behind her and she felt his breath on her
neck. Her fingers curled into tight fists. "We'll be more careful," he agreed, dropping a kiss on the nape of her neck and
slipping his hands around her waist.

Freddie darted out of his embrace. She shook her head and

spun around and wrapped her arms across her breasts. "No. We can't."

"What do you mean, we can't? Can't what?"

"Can't…that." Freddie couldn't say it. Wouldn't let herself say it! She shook her head again, angry at herself for having let things get that far. "We can't," she repeated.

"Can't…kiss?" He sounded somewhere between amused and incredulous.

She steeled herself against him. "That's right."

"Can't…touch?"

"No."

He cocked his head. "Why not?"

As if she could give him a logical reason! "Because…because…it won't do!"

"Oh for God's sake! Don't do that 'lady of the manor' act. 'It won't do,'" he mocked theatrically. "Why the hell not? You want me. I want you!"

Fortunately, before Freddie could blurt out, "Yes," she managed a split second's thought.

"Our bodies," she began with the precision of a governess splitting hairs, "are not the sum of us. While our bodies might wish closer contact, our minds, our hearts, our souls…feel otherwise."

"Mine doesn't." Gabe looked straight at her with his clear blue gaze.

Freddie turned away. She hugged herself tighter. "Well, mine does."

She couldn't want him—couldn't *love* him! Because that's what it would mean if her heart and mind and soul felt the same way her body clearly did.

And he didn't love her, either.

It was just that she was here. She was handy. He didn't have anyone else. What would be an evening's recreation for him would be a blow to the heart for her.

Determinedly Freddie shook her head again. "No," she repeated. "Please. It was a…a mistake."

"Was it?" Gabe didn't move, just stood there looking at her. His hands hung loosely at his sides. And then, as if he couldn't help it, he reached for her. "Freddie." His voice was soft but insistent. Urgent. Beseeching.

She shook her bowed head resolutely. "No, Gabe. Please. Don't ask me."

His hands dropped, but still he didn't move.

Finally she made herself look up at him, meet his gaze. "You said real cowboys follow orders, do what they're supposed to."

"And we're not supposed to touch each other?" he challenged her.

Their gazes locked.

Gabe stood there, not even breathing while Freddie held her breath, too, and prayed for the strength to resist.

Resist. Resist.

She managed to shake her head. "No. We're not. This is...tempting. But it's not... It's too...dangerous."

"Dangerous." He repeated the word as if he was trying it on for size. He seemed to chew on it a bit, then his mouth curved bitterly at one corner. "Final word?"

One last chance. *Are you going to grab it, Freddie?* she asked herself. "Final word," she muttered.

"Whatever you say, Fred." And he turned and walked out the door.

In the morning he called Earl. "I'm outa here."

The old man coughed, sounding like he'd choked on a crumpet. "Gabe? Is that you? For God's sake, man, what's going on down there? Every time I ring your office some snippy little pigeon tells me you're too busy to come to the telephone!"

So, Beatrice had learned. Well, good. Gabe supposed he was glad.

It was what he'd come for, wasn't it? To turn things around.

"What did you say?" Earl demanded. "What are you out of?"

"Here," Gabe said flatly. "I've been here six weeks. That's long enough."

Earl made a disapproving clucking sound. "Well, I suppose

I shouldn't be dismayed. You lasted longer than I thought even if you didn't get the job done.''

"I *got* the job done!''

He told his grandfather he'd remedied the lack of local news. He told him about his new correspondents—Mrs. Peek and her cohorts from the Women's Institute. He told the old man that the local touch brought back a bit of advertising. Beatrice, given a shot of confidence, had helped out enormously.

"They're advertising with us now," Gabe said. "Revenues have increased sixfold."

"Sixfold?'' Earl was gasping for air.

"So far. It's a risk, admittedly. If they don't see an increase in business from the ads, chances are they won't keep it up after six months or so. But I've got six-month commitments out of most of them. That ought to give whoever you bring in a chance to solidify things.''

"That fellow Percy—''

"Not Percy," Gabe said. "Not if you want it to work.''

"Really?'' Earl was intrigued. "Who would you suggest?''

"Beatrice. The one who wouldn't let you talk to me.''

"The secretary?'' Earl sputtered.

"She keeps the office running. She's a quick study. She knows which side her bread is buttered on. She understands the business side of things. And she makes a damn fine cup of coffee." She'd demanded that he teach her.

"Humph. Coffee? Ugh. Beatrice, eh? I'll think about it," he said. "I want all these recommendations on paper. I want a rundown of all the figures since you arrived. I want a starting point and a current update.''

"I'll fax them to you.''

"Bring them. You're coming to see me before you leave certainly. Aren't you?''

Was he?

Gabe guessed he was. He would have preferred to simply hightail it right out of the country without having to undergo Earl's scrutiny. But who knew when he'd see the old badger again? And he wanted the satisfaction of showing his grandfather he'd done far better than the old man had expected, didn't he?

Of course he did.

But mostly he wanted to be gone.

He didn't want to have to sit across the table from Freddie any longer and look at the woman who wanted him with her body but not with her heart and soul. He didn't want to see her, to listen to her, to talk to her.

There was no point, damn it!

"When are you coming?" Earl asked.

"Soon," Gabe promised. "By the end of the week for sure."

She shouldn't have been surprised when he said he was leaving.

He'd ridden in, rescued the *Gazette,* and was about to ride off into the sunset. It was exactly what cowboys did.

All the same, she felt as if she'd been punched in the stomach when he said he'd be leaving on Friday.

Both Charlie and Emma looked positively stricken. Then Charlie said hopefully, "Just to go to London? To see your grandfather?"

"I'm stopping there," Gabe agreed. "Then I'm going home. To Montana." His tone was firm, his words determined, but he didn't look at any of them.

After the first instant Freddie didn't look at him either. She saw Charlie swallow and Emma bite her lip. It was all she could do not to bite her own. At the same time, she told herself it was just as well.

Better than having him hanging around. Smiling at her. Teasing her.

Tempting her.

She didn't know how long she would be able to resist him on a daily basis. The memories of a night of loving Gabe McBride might be wonderful, but he made no promises—they had no future.

Not that she wanted one.

He was like Mark—a man who took risks.

Freddie couldn't risk. Not again. She couldn't even let herself love him and cherish the memories. They would never be enough.

"But I don't want him to go," Emma said plaintively that night when Freddie was tucking her up in bed. Her lower lip stuck out and she looked pleadingly at her mother.

"You knew he was going to. He only came to get the newspaper sorted out, that's all," Freddie said firmly.

"Doesn't have to be all," Charlie said from the doorway where he slouched in his pajamas, arms folded across his chest. "He could stay. You could ask him to stay."

"I could do no such thing, Charles Crossman! I would never!"

"Well, you ought to," Charlie said stubbornly. "He'd be a good father."

As much as she wanted to, Freddie couldn't deny that. But she pressed her lips into a tight line. "He's not interested in being a father." And even if he were, he was not the man she would choose.

"He likes us," Emma maintained. "He likes kids. He said so."

"I'm sure he does. And perhaps someday he'll have his own," Freddie said, and was surprised how much the thought hurt.

"But not us." With one last accusing look at his mother, Charlie slumped back to his own room.

Freddie stared after him, feeling equal parts dismayed and helpless. *Try to understand,* she wanted to implore him. But she knew it was pointless.

He was a child. He wanted a father.

Gabe was handy. Gabe was fun. He was a little boy's ideal.

But that didn't make it possible.

They roped the cow until it was cross-eyed every day for the rest of the week.

They sang "The Streets of Laredo" and "The Yellow Rose of Texas" and "The Double Diamond" and every other cowboy song Gabe knew.

They watched movies—westerns every one. *Shane. Stage-*

coach. Red River. All by popular demand. Charlie and Emma's demand. They couldn't get enough. And Gabe was quite willing to give it to them.

He was annoyed at Freddie, angry that she'd rebuffed him, hurt, if the truth were known. At least he guessed that's what that aching feeling somewhere in his midsection meant.

He didn't like being toyed with, tempted, led on—and then told to take a hike.

She was chicken. Afraid of him—of her feelings for him.

He wasn't afraid of his feelings for her. He hadn't even really thought about them. Feelings weren't something Gabe was very good at. Not analyzing them, anyhow. If he felt something, he damn sure wouldn't turn his back on it like Ms. Frederica Crossman!

Well, the heck with her.

But not with her children. He had a few more days to spend with them, and he was going to be sure they knew that life was worth living, that risks were worth taking.

"You guys are doin' great," he told them.

"I never met a better cowgirl," he told Emma. "Not even Claire," he added, fingers crossed, and was sure Claire wouldn't mind if she ever saw the way Emma beamed.

"You just keep pluggin' and someday you'll make a hand," he told the boy.

"A hand?" Charlie echoed.

"A good cowboy," Gabe translated.

Charlie grinned. "Like you."

Charlie believed in him. Emma believed in him. Beatrice believed in him.

So, grudgingly, did Percy Pomfret-Mumphrey, over his dead body. Even Earl seemed to believe in him at the moment. Everyone believed in him but Freddie.

"Right," he said firmly. "You be a cowboy like me."

"An' ride bulls," Charlie said.

"Definitely," Gabe agreed, glad the kid wasn't a chicken like his mother.

Charlie cocked his head. "Do all cowboys ride bulls?"

"Only the best." He winked. "No. Only rodeo cowboys,"

he said. "And not all of them. I didn't start out ridin' 'em, either. I started out ridin' sheep."

"*Sheep?*" Both children stared.

"When I was a boy. Mutton bustin' we called it."

Charlie looked speculatively out across the field beyond the long-suffering cow. He ran his tongue over his lips. "I'd like to try that. Do you think Mr. Bolt would mind?"

Actually Gabe didn't. He'd had a chat with Josiah Bolt when he and Beatrice were doing their rounds of shopkeepers and had met him in the hardware store. Josiah had actually laughed at Gabe's tale of them roping his sheep.

"Come on," he said now, seizing on the idea. One last thrill.

They found the sheep in Bolt's field near the road. And while Gabe held one big ewe steady and kept her next to the hedgerow, Charlie clambered up and settled down onto her back. His eyes were wide with excitement, his cheeks bright red.

"All set?" Gabe asked. Then with one hand he reached up and took off his Stetson and settled it on the little boy's head.

Charlie looked up at it, then at Gabe, awe-struck.

Gabe grinned. "For luck," he said and tugged it down until Charlie barely peeked out.

The boy grinned. Then, lips tight, knuckles white, he nodded.

"Let 'er rip!" Gabe let go and gave the ewe a light smack. She bolted across the field with Charlie clinging fiercely to her back.

Darn good thing Freddie had gone to town. She would be having a fit right now if she could see her first born hurtling across the field clutching the back of a good-sized ewe with both hands while he yelled "Yeehaw!" at the top of his lungs.

"Ride 'em, cowboy!" Gabe whooped.

Charlie rode. The sheep careened through the field, but Charlie stuck tight. Not until it swerved right and plunged down a sharp hill did Charlie, still shrieking, crash to the ground.

"*Charlie!*"

Gabe spun around to see Freddie getting out of her car. She scrambled over the wall, then ran toward them, hair streaming behind her, face stark white with terror. "Charlie!"

Gabe started toward her, then turned and went to Charlie

instead. "He's all right!" he called over his shoulder. "He's just had the wind knocked out of him."

Charlie, still gasping, tried to struggle up. There was blood on the boy's lip, and his face looked a little blue from lack of air. Gabe knelt beside him and patted Charlie's ribs.

"Hurt anywhere?" he asked, keeping his body between Charlie and his mother.

"N-no," Charlie managed. "P-pretty g-good, huh? Huh, Gabe?"

But before Gabe could reply, Freddie swooped in, practically knocking him out of the way. "Dear God, Charlie! Are you all right?"

The boy gulped, started to answer, apparently realized a stutter wouldn't do, and swallowed, to nod wordlessly instead. He swiped a sleeve quickly across his bloody lip.

Freddie started to gather him close, but the boy squirmed away. "M'all right, Mum!"

"He is," Gabe agreed.

Freddie whirled on him. "Like you'd care! What were you trying to do? Kill him?"

"*Kill him?* He was riding a sheep, that's all. Bustin' mutton."

"Busting his head, more like!" Her hands were trembling. She made fists of them quickly, then opened them again, shook them out. She glared at him, her normally rosy complexion ash white. Then taking a deep shuddering breath, she turned to Charlie. "That's enough. No more sheep."

"But—"

"Come along. We're going home. Now."

"He wasn't hurt," Gabe intervened. "Not much, anyway," he added, determined to be perfectly honest. "And it isn't as if he's the only kid to ever bust a mutton. Other kids do it. An' he wanted to ride one."

"It doesn't matter what he wanted! I'm his mother! I say what he does. Not him! Not you!" She had Charlie on his feet now and was steering him toward her car.

Gabe kept pace. "You've got to let him try things, Fred. You can't keep him wrapped up in cotton wool his whole life!"

"I can do whatever I want! I'm his mother. You're...you're...a cowboy! Here today. Gone tomorrow. *Passing through!*" Her eyes were flashing, her hair was wild, her breasts were heaving beneath her jacket. She was beautiful and tempting.

And right.

He was passing through.

He had no say. Charlie wasn't his. He had no rights.

Not unless she gave them to him.

Fat chance.

"Fine," he said after a long moment. He shrugged with all the nonchalance he could muster. He reached down and snagged his hat off the ground. "Have it your way, Fred. Teach your children that risks are bad, that it's always better to play it safe."

He set it on his head, then gave the brim a tug. "I wouldn't. If they were mine, they'd learn to be cowboys—in the best sense of the word."

There was apparently nothing in the bill of sale of the *Buckworthy Gazette* that prevented Percy from quitting, which was exactly what he did when Gabe promoted Beatrice to office manager on his last day at work.

"Me?" Beatrice said, astonished.

"Her?" Percy gasped, appalled.

"That's right," Gabe said to both of them. "That way I'm sure the paper will be in good hands."

And he wanted it in good hands. The *Gazette* was the one thing he had done right, the one thing he was happy about.

The only thing that mattered, he told himself. It was why he had come, after all.

Freddie had been...Freddie had been a distraction. Beautiful. Lively. Tempting. Fun.

Annoying. Irritating. Downright infuriating.

It was a damn good thing he was going home.

He knew Freddie felt the same way.

For the rest of the week, they steered clear of each other. She fixed his dinner, but she declined any help with the washing up. She sat in the room and read while he told the children stories, but she never joined in. She didn't come and sit in the parlor with him after the children were in bed, either. She never let herself be alone with him.

Because she was chicken.

Well, fine. If that's the way she wanted it, it didn't matter to him.

They barely spoke all week. He thought they might not speak at all, that he might just get in his car and drive off and she'd never say a word.

But when he came in from work his last afternoon, she handed him a stack of clean folded laundry and said in proper landlady-ish tones, "I think that's everything then."

Everything.

All that had passed between them in these few weeks—all the joy, all the laughter, all the smiles, the looks, the touches, the kiss—had all come down to nothing more than a stack of laundry.

He looked at her. She was already on her way back to the kitchen.

"Thanks," he muttered.

He carried the clean clothes back to his room and began packing his bag. He moved slowly, deliberately. He'd put off packing so he could visit with the kids while he did it. He'd expected them to be waiting for him when he got home this afternoon. But the house had been empty except for Freddie.

"Where are they?" he'd asked when he came in.

She'd shrugged vaguely. "They went off to play somewhere." Her tone had been dismissive, almost airy.

Gabe knew she was glad, grateful they weren't hovering over him, stretching things out, asking for one last story. It proved how little he mattered to them. He could see the satisfaction in her eyes.

He'd nodded, certain then that they'd be back before he left.

But it took him ten minutes to pack. Now he was done.

He stripped the bed, tossed the sheets in the wash, folded the duvet, packed, then repacked his bag. He couldn't wait much longer.

He had told his grandfather he'd be there late tonight so he needed to get moving. Reluctantly he zipped the duffel and picked up his jacket, then headed for the door. Turning, he took one last look back at the room, memorizing it.

Why? he asked himself savagely. *So you can drag out the memory and think about it when you're back home where you belong? So you can remember all those nights in that lonely bed? So you can recall hopes dashed and dreams thwarted? So you can miss Freddie and the kids?*

"Oh yeah. Good idea," he mocked himself.

He didn't need this. He didn't need *them.* Not any of them. Not Freddie who had wanted him and insisted she didn't. Not her children who clamored to be cowboys, but who, the minute he said he was leaving, vanished, not caring a whit.

He shoved his arms into his jacket, then grabbed the duffel and headed down the stairs. Freddie was in the kitchen, peeling potatoes at the sink. From the stiffness of her shoulders, he knew she'd been listening for him…waiting.

"I'm going now," he said brusquely. "Tell the kids I said goodbye."

"Yes." She turned, blinked, swallowed, smiled. Her smile looked just a little strained.

Gabe felt a small measure of satisfaction. He smiled back, a polite, distant smile—the sort you gave the innkeeper who'd made your stay pleasant. He headed out the door. "Watch out for runaway rabbits," he said over his shoulder.

"What? Oh—" She managed a little laugh. But she followed him out at least and stood on the porch to watch him go.

They stared at each other again. No laundry between them now.

The "everything" no longer reduced to that—the memories, the might-have-beens crowding in, piling up.

Then in the stillness, Gabe heard the sudden pounding of swift footsteps coming down the gravel drive.

"Mummy! Mummy! Gabe!" It was Emma, feet flying, cheeks blazing. "Come quick! Charlie's gone up to Dawes's field to ride the bull!"

Five

It was Freddie's worst nightmare.

Worse than her worst nightmare. So bad—so fraught with the potential for disaster—that she would never let herself think or dream about such a thing! She was frozen where she stood.

"Come on!" Gabe was grabbing her hand and towing her to the car. "Show me where they are," he commanded Emma. "And tell me what the hell is going on?"

"Heck," Freddie corrected faintly. But as her fingers knotted and her heart lodged in her throat, she really thought hell felt more like it.

Emma pointed the way. "Ch-Charlie...thought it would... be a good idea," she told Gabe, her words coming in bursts as she gulped enough air to say them. "T-to prove he could do it. S-so you'd t-take us w-with you!"

"Jesus!" Gabe let out a sharp exhalation of breath. "Your mother told you—"

"But if he p-proved it—if he did it—she wouldn't have to

worry a-anymore,'' Emma cut him off determinedly. She gave Freddie a look that was both nervous and defiant. "Charlie said so!''

That wasn't how it worked, Freddie wanted to tell her. Mothers worried. It went with the role. Sometimes—since Mark had died—worrying seemed to define her role. For all the good it had done. Her fingers knotted tighter.

Please God, don't let anything happen to Charlie.

They were almost to Dawes's field now. Freddie could see Mrs. Peek's old bicycle propped against the hedgerow.

"What's Mrs. Peek doing here?" Gabe demanded.

"She came up while I was sitting on the wall waiting for Charlie. An' she never just goes by, you know. She always stops to talk. An' she asked what I was doing. An' I thought...I thought maybe she'd write a story about it, about Charlie being so brave an' all and then we could send it to you an' you'd come back an'... She told me to go get you quick. She said she was going to try to find Charlie before the bull did.''

Gabe leapt out of the car. "Wait here!''

"I'm coming!'' Freddie was hot on his heels when he stopped suddenly and she slammed right into him.

"No,'' he said fiercely, "you're not! The last thing we need is somebody else out wandering around in that field. I can't take care of all of you. You stay here with Emma. She seems to be the only one with any sense.'' He flicked Emma a quick strained grin, then focused again on Freddie. "You're staying, got that?''

"I—''

"Just say you've got it. You're the one who doesn't take risks, remember? Don't change your mind now.''

"But—''

"Got it. Say, I've got it.''

"I've got it,'' Freddie said desperately, frantically. She knew Gabe was right, even though every maternal instinct wanted to insist it was her duty—not his—to go after Charlie. "Stop wasting time badgering me! Just find Charlie and get him out of there!''

* * *

Gabe had been scared a few times in his life—the first time he'd ridden a bull, the night his father had had a heart attack, the day his mother said, "I guess we'll have to sell the ranch if you don't want to run it."

He'd been scared enough of his inadequacies never to have done any rodeo bullfighting at all. And he quaked in his boots whenever he heard his name mentioned along with the words *commitment* and *marriage*.

But he'd never been as scared as he was now.

A boy—a *little* boy!—was out looking for a bull to ride.

Because of him.

A little boy might get trampled, gored—*killed!*—because of him!

Because Charlie worshiped him. Because he wanted to be like him. Because Gabe had opened his big mouth and said he wouldn't coddle his children.

"If they were mine, they'd learn to be cowboys," he'd said after the sheep-riding fiasco, like he knew everything, like he had all the answers, like he was some blinkin' god!

Gabe's relationship with the Almighty was casual, but steady. Any man who rode bulls for a living and courted disaster on a daily basis was generally on speaking terms with God.

Gabe spoke now. He murmured one prayer after another as he strode across the field, eyes darting this way and that, looking for Charlie's navy anorak or Mrs. Peek's red sweater or, in the best of all worlds, neither of them—only the bull.

"I didn't mean it," he told God. "Well, maybe I did. But I was only trying to help. I don't want her raisin' 'em to be sissies. I never meant for him to do somethin' dumb. So take care of him, huh? And You damned—er, darned—well better take care of Mrs. Peek, too!"

As he crested the hill, he glanced back once to see Freddie and Emma perched on the wall, arms hugged across their chests, eyes intent on him. He wished he could yell back that he'd found them, but the field rolled on, trees and rock outcroppings scattered here and there.

No Charlie. No Mrs. Peek. No bull.

Gabe hurried on, yelling Charlie's name as he went, then stopping to listen for a response.

And then he saw the bull.

Huge, brown and mud-caked, the animal was pacing agitatedly between two beech trees, twitching his tail, snorting and huffing and pawing the ground.

Gabe stopped dead. He looked around for Charlie or Mrs. Peek and was relieved not to see either of them.

Then he heard Charlie's voice. "Gabe! Hi, Gabe! We're up here!"

Gabe looked around desperately. But he only saw the field, the rocks, the trees. And, of course, the bull.

Then a leg dangled down from one of the trees. "Here! In the trees."

Suddenly the other beech shook, too. A pair of dark brown brogans and heavy woolen stockings appeared.

Mrs. Peek had climbed a tree?

The bull spotted her legs and snorted. It whuffled, blew and charged.

"Look out!" Gabe yelled.

The legs disappeared up into the branches just as the bull crashed against the tree. The ground beneath Gabe's feet trembled. He muttered an imprecation under his breath, looking around wildly for inspiration.

And for a refuge, as the bull, after having hit the tree, turned around and spotted him.

Gabe remembered a rodeo clown buddy who said, "Time slows down when I fight a bull."

As far as Gabe was concerned, it never slowed down enough for him to be sure he'd get out of the way. That was why he'd never tried bullfighting.

He was going to have to try it now.

He'd have to attract the bull, entice it, get it to run at him and away from Mrs. Peek and Charlie. It was the only way they could escape.

Slowly, keeping an eye on the bull, Gabe pulled off his jacket. If the bull got it, ripped it out of his hands, he'd move on to the hat. If it got the hat—well, he wouldn't let himself think that far ahead.

He didn't think about what would happen if the bull got him instead of the jacket, either. He flapped the jacket, moving away from the trees. The bull was curious, but not enthralled. He looked back at Mrs. Peek's shoes.

"Use our sweater!" Mrs. Peek called. "Us was tryin' to distract 'im with it. It's down there." A hand dipped down below the branches of the tree and pointed.

Gabe looked and, sure enough, he spotted her faded red sweater lying on the ground.

"Us'll divert his attention," she called.

"Right." He wasn't going to argue. She was reasonably safe in the tree, and the bull was once more looking her way.

Mrs. Peek lowered her legs again. She kicked them. She waggled them. She called, "Yooo-hooo, *toro!* Over here!"

The bull snorted and turned in her direction. Warily Gabe moved to snatch up the sweater. Then, clutching it, he shouted and waved it in the direction of the bull.

The bull stopped. It stared.

Deliberately Gabe flapped the sweater again. He started walking slowly parallel to the bull, away from the trees...trying to get the bull to charge.

One second it was staring. The next it was racing toward him. And Gabe learned it was true, what his buddy had said.

Though it all happened in the blink of an eye, somehow Gabe saw every step, every ball of mud the bull's hooves flung high.

He waved the sweater, flimsy and insubstantial, out to his side and leapt back as—whoosh—the bull pounded past.

Breathing like each gulp would be his last, Gabe side-stepped, moving even farther from the trees. If he could get behind them and the bull came after him, they would be left in the clear.

He moved. He flapped the sweater. He said, "Come on, you big fat son-of-a-gun. Let's see how fast you can run."

Not all that fast, please God, he prayed.

Once more the bull charged. Gabe dodged, stumbling this

time, falling to one knee and wincing as the bull skidded and turned to come at him again.

Desperate, Gabe staggered to his feet.

"Come on! Come on! A miss is as good as a mile!" He'd twisted his knee as he fell, the same knee he'd hurt more times than he could count when he'd ridden bulls. He gritted his teeth as the pain stabbed him. "Come on!"

The bull came. It lowered its head and charged—and snagged the sweater, ripping it out of his hands.

But at least he was behind the trees now, across the meadow away from Charlie and Mrs. Peek.

Beyond the bull, Gabe saw Charlie swing down out of the tree. As the bull came at him once more, Mrs. Peek descended, too. They glanced in his direction.

"Go on!" Gabe yelled. "Go!"

And the instant before he had to spin away, he saw Mrs. Peek grab Charlie's hand and run with him up the hill.

Once they were out of sight, Gabe took a breath.

And panicked.

He had no sweater, he'd dropped his jacket before the bull had made its first pass. It turned at the hedgerow by the far end of the field and looked back at him.

Two-thousand pounds of muscle and horn and meanness was all that stood between him and safety.

All?

Gabe almost laughed.

He took off his hat. Slowly he flapped it up and down. He took a step, then another, moving toward the bull this time, not away.

"Come and get me," he said softly. "Come on. Once more. You've only got one more shot, buddy. Miss one more time and I'm outa here."

Get me and I'm outa here, too. In a box.

The bull lowered its head. It snorted. It pawed.

It ran straight at him.

"She was amazing," Charlie was babbling with admiration. "Just like one of them bull fighters on the telly!"

Freddie had her arms around both of them, hugging them, almost sobbing in relief. "Thank you," she said. "Thank you. Thank you. If you hadn't—I don't know what I'd have done if—"

But Mrs. Peek shushed her before she could even speak the unspeakable. "Us gave 'im a little breathing room," the older woman said modestly. "Us'd still be sittin' up in those trees if it weren't for your Mr. McBride."

Mr. McBride. Gabe.

Freddie looked around frantically. "Where—"

"He's fighting the bull, Mum!"

Oh, God. She remembered when Gabe and the children had been watching the rodeo videos. Emma had been fascinated with the bullfighting clowns.

"Were you ever one of them?" she'd asked Gabe eagerly.

"Not on your life, sweetheart. There are some things even I'm not fool enough to tackle."

But today he was.

Freddie closed her eyes. "Oh, Gabe. Oh my God, Gabe." She hugged her arms across her chest. She wanted to vault the hedgerow and race down the meadow and scream his name, demand that he come. And she knew she didn't dare.

She knew there was no point. She would cause more trouble. As if he needed more trouble....

"Gabe!" Charlie shouted.

"Gabe!" shrieked Emma.

And Freddie opened her eyes, looking down the field wildly—and in vain.

Then she looked where her children were looking—where Charlie was running—and saw Gabe, dirty, disheveled, but—thank God—in one piece, coming up the lane toward them.

She started toward him, then stopped, watching as Charlie hurled himself into Gabe's arms. She saw those arms go hard around him, saw Gabe crush the boy against his chest and bury his face in Charlie's hair.

"Don't ever—don't you *ever*—do a thing like that again!" His voice was ragged as he let the boy down, but kept a hand on him.

"I only wanted to ride 'im," Charlie said. "You do."

"It's different," Gabe said, his voice still rough. "Way different."

"But—"

Gabe put his arm around Charlie's narrow shoulders. "Listen," he said. "You don't have to prove yourself to me or to anyone." Then, with his arm still around her son, he looked up at Freddie. "I'm sorry."

It was the last thing she expected him to say. "S-sorry?"

He nodded. "He did it because of what I said, that I wouldn't coddle them. I'm sorry. I had no right."

"It's…it's all right," Freddie's voice faltered. "He's all right. *You're* all right." She wanted to go to him, to put her arms around him the way he had around Charlie, to hug him, to prove to herself he was all in one piece, safe. Alive.

She gave him a watery smile, praying that she wouldn't be soppy and start crying. She was trembling all over.

"All's well, ends well," Mrs. Peek said. "An' what a story us'll have!" She rubbed her hands together and her eyes sparkled with excitement.

But Gabe shook his head. "I'm writing this one."

Her face fell.

"And we'll have Dodd the photo out to take your picture."

"*Our* picture?" Mrs. Peek blinked owlishly.

Gabe grinned and put his other arm around her. "If it hadn't been for you, Charlie's adventure with the bull might have turned out a heck of a lot worse. In next Thursday's edition we'll have a story—and a picture. This time, Mrs. Peek, you're the news!"

He knew words didn't change things.

Yes, Charlie was safe. But he had been at risk. He might have been killed or seriously injured out there.

It was all his fault, and Gabe knew it.

Even though Freddie smiled and said it wasn't, she was very quiet all the way home. She tried not to fuss over Charlie—Gabe could see that. But he could also see that she had to almost forcibly keep herself from touching him, patting him, stroking his hair. And every time she turned away from Charlie to look at him, almost instantly her gaze skated away again.

As if she couldn't bear to look at him.

Well, she wouldn't have to. Not much longer.

He should have left at once, but he needed a shower. He needed to put on some of those clean clothes she'd washed and folded for him. He couldn't turn up at Earl's looking like he'd just stepped out of the rodeo arena. He didn't want to have to explain.

By the time he'd cleaned up, though, Freddie had supper on the table.

"Please," she said, "eat with us,"

And the children said, "Please, Gabe."

Truth be told, he didn't want to say no. All the momentum that was supposed to have got him out the door had vanished in the field. All the adrenaline that had kept him going was gone.

It was a simple meal. Pork chops. A lettuce salad. Bread and butter.

It was the best meal he'd ever eaten.

It stuck in his throat.

Because in just a few minutes—an hour at most—he was going to have to leave it all behind—leave this house, these children.

This woman.

He watched her every move. Every time she turned away, his eyes followed her. They traced her steps, her shape, her smile. She smiled at the children. Once or twice she even spared a smile for him. He memorized them, stored them away for the not too distant future when those memories would be all he had.

"Tell us a story, Gabe," Emma begged after dinner was over and the dishes were done.

"I—" He was going to say he couldn't, that he had to leave. But he couldn't get the words past his throat.

It would be easier, he told himself, to go if the kids were in bed asleep, not standing there watching him drive away. So he said, "I know a short one."

"About bulls?" Emma asked.

Gabe saw Charlie shudder. "No," he told the little girl. "This one's about a lord."

Out of the corner of his eye, he saw Freddie start. But he deliberately didn't look at her.

He sat down with the children and began his tale. He told them about a pair of cousins—"blood brothers"— because once upon a time they'd pricked their fingers and mingled their already shared blood and promised they would always look out for each other. But then they grew up and grew apart.

One went to be a cowboy. The other was groomed to be an earl.

"Tell us about the cowboy," Emma begged.

But Gabe shook his head. "You know all about the cowboy."

He told them about Randall instead. He told them about duty and responsibility and commitment. He told them about putting other people's needs first and sticking to what needed to be done.

"Sometimes it isn't much fun. And it doesn't always look heroic, but it is," he said. "Just like Mrs. Peek—doing what she always did—but she might have saved your life today."

"You saved my life," Charlie insisted. "You fought the bull."

"I wouldn't have even known where you were if Mrs. Peek hadn't sent Emma to get us."

"But still—"

Gabe shook his head. "I'm no hero."

He glanced at Freddie, hoping she heard.

She was sitting on the far side of the room, the mending in her lap. She didn't come and sit down to listen. He didn't blame her.

He hoped, though, that she heard enough of what he was telling them that she would know how much he regretted what had happened.

He said, "You remember that story even if you forget all the rest." Then he stood up. "Time for bed."

Charlie hugged him fiercely. Emma said, "Don't go, Gabe. Don't go."

But as he gave her a goodnight kiss, he said, "I have to."

They went upstairs and he gave them each a last hug, then left Freddie to say her goodnights to them. He went back down and stood for just a minute, looking around, letting it all seep in. The memories. The children. The woman.

Then he picked up his duffel bags once more.

"Gabe?"

He turned. Freddie stood on the stairs. She looked pale, fragile. Breakable. Hurt—because of him.

"Please. Wait."

He didn't want to wait. Didn't know how much more he could stand.

But Freddie came down the stairs. Her fingers knotted together. "You said you were sorry. But I'm the one who should be saying it. It's just... I think about Mark. He did foolish things. Risky things. He...died! Charlie..."

She broke off. The tears that had been threatening since the moment Emma had pounded up the drive with the news spilled over now. She put her hands to her face. "Oh, help."

He had no choice. He dropped the duffel and went to her. "Charlie didn't die," he said thickly. "And he won't try it again. He won't do what Mark did, either. He'll learn. We all do stupid stuff as boys. It's part of the definition." He took hold of her arms, but that didn't seem enough, so he wrapped them around her, drew her in. "He was up a tree, Freddie. Scared, but safe. He learned his lesson."

"But you...you could have..."

"I should have gone up the tree, too," Gabe said wryly, "but I didn't want you having to call out the fire brigade. How would that have looked? What a British version of a cowboy I would have been!"

He saw the faintest hint of a smile touch her mouth. She looked up into his eyes. "You're a wonderful cowboy. The best. Thank you."

He snorted softly. "Don't know what you're thanking me for."

"You saved Charlie. And—" she faltered for a second "—you taught me a lesson, too."

He looked at her blankly.

Freddie went up on tiptoe. "That there are some risks worth taking," she whispered and she touched her lips to his.

He only meant to comfort her. Truly. He only wanted to share on a deeper level all that they had shared today.

It was, perhaps, the one time in his life he'd held a beautiful woman in his arms and had not been hoping for more.

But somehow comforting and sharing turned to touching, to caressing, to kissing, to loving. And when Freddie took his hand and led him back up the stairs to her room, he didn't say no.

He'd wanted her forever. Couldn't remember a time when he hadn't gone to sleep thinking of Freddie Crossman and awakened with thoughts of her in his mind.

But still he had to ask. "Are you sure you know what you're doing?"

The last thing he wanted was to have her wish it had never happened. "You've been under a lot of stress. You're overwrought because of what almost happened to Charlie."

"I've never been more sure of anything in my life." And then she looped her arms around his neck and kissed him again.

There was tenderness in this kiss—as there had been in the earlier one. But now there was desire, too.

Gabe knew about desire. Knew about desperation. His whole body seemed to throb with it, with his need of her.

"Freddie," he warned, voice shaking as he gave her one last chance. He still had—he hoped—a thread of control.

Until she tugged his shirt loose from his waistband and slid her hands up underneath, caressing his heated flesh, making the blood pound in his veins. And he was gone. Lost.

He kissed her hungrily, eagerly. His fingers fumbled with the buttons on her shirt. She made quicker work of his, then peeled the shirt off his shoulders and ran her hands over his

chest. Then, as if she hadn't already lit his fire, she pressed a dozen tiny kisses here and there.

He muttered. He stumbled trying to shed his jeans and get out of his boots. With her hands Freddie both soothed and excited him.

"Shhh," she whispered. "I'm not going anywhere." And if there was the barest hint of emphasis on the word *I*, Gabe wasn't sure he hadn't imagined it. But in any case, it was true. *He* was the one who would be leaving.

But not now. Later.

In the morning.

Not yet.

They tumbled onto the bed, and then, as if by some unspoken accord, their movements slowed, became languid, their touches gentled.

Gabe was no young buck, desperate to fulfill his body's urgings. He wanted her, yes, desperately. But he could take his time—enjoy, appreciate, savor the softness, the smoothness, the suppleness that was Freddie Crossman.

He stretched out on the bed and leaned up on one elbow to survey her.

"Yes," he whispered. "Ah, yes." With one finger he traced a line from the tip of her nose across her lips to her chin, then down between her breasts. His fingers lingered there. His mouth touched there. Freddie shivered. She clutched at him.

"Gabe!" Her voice was urgent, needy.

He smiled. But it was a strained smile because he was needy, too. Needing Freddie. He kissed each breast. His fingers moved down, found her—slick and soft and ready for him. She squirmed under his touch.

He shut his eyes. Bit his lip. Held his breath.

"Come to me, Gabe!" She reached for him, ran her hands over him, found the hottest, hardest part of him, making him exhale harshly.

"Freddie!"

"Now, Gabe," she urged. And then she brought him home.

That was what it felt like. Home. Where he was warm and safe and loved. Home—where he belonged.

Sex had always been fun for Gabe. It had never made him want to weep before. Now it did.

For love. For joy. For the pure unadulterated beauty of the way they fit together—body and soul.

And then because even that could be better—and he knew it—he began to move. Slowly at first. Savoring every second. Making himself wait. Making Freddie wait. Watching her in the moonlight. Watching the way her lips parted, the way her back arched and her body trembled. Feeling the way her body tightened around him.

And then his concentration shattered. He shattered, too. Right along with her.

He had never been more broken. He'd never felt more whole.

She had no willpower.

A stronger woman would have been able to resist. A stronger woman would have thanked Gabe McBride for saving her son's life—then waved him goodbye and breathed a sigh of relief when he went away.

Not Freddie. Not now. Not tonight.

Tonight, God help her, she needed his touch. She needed his warmth. She needed *him!*

It was true, what she'd told him. In those awful moments when she hadn't known where he was—if the bull had spared Charlie and gored Gabe—she'd felt an awful despair, a wrenching sadness, a hollow sense of loss.

For whatever they could have had.

For what might have been.

She didn't expect forever. She knew better.

When she'd married Mark, she'd expected forever. She'd counted on it. And she'd been devastated by his death. She'd fought to protect Charlie and Emma from any such risks. She'd hoped—by refusing to get involved with anyone else—to protect herself from further pain.

She was past that now. She knew better.

There was no way to protect oneself from pain. There was

no life without it. There was just pretended indifference. She knew now that was worse.

To let Gabe go without loving him would be worse.

She knew he was going back to Montana. In the morning he would be gone. But at least she would have tonight. And if the memories caused her heartache, they couldn't be worse than the fear and anguish she'd felt before she'd known he was safe.

She lay now, watching him sleep, and reached out to tug the duvet up around his shoulders. At her movement, he smiled faintly. He reached out an arm and drew her close.

Tears pricking behind her eyelids, Freddie snuggled in. A ragged breath caught in her throat. She pressed a kiss against his jaw. "I love you," she whispered.

He didn't hear her.

It was just as well.

Gabe didn't get out before the kids got up.

He was, thank heavens, *not* still in their mother's bedroom. But he wasn't out the door yet, either. It had been too wonderful lying in bed with her, too tempting to stay just a little longer, to make each kiss last, but not *the* last.

But then Freddie had heard Emma padding around and she'd almost bolted out of bed, grabbing for her robe as she did so.

"They can't—" she hissed. "They can't find you in here!"

"They won't," Gabe swore. But even after she'd disappeared into the bathroom, he lay there a moment longer, just breathing, looking, touching—taking it all in.

Then he dragged himself up and pulled on his clothes. He made the bed. Found a single long hair on Freddie's pillow. He curled it around his finger, then touched it to his lips.

He wanted— He needed…

"Will you get out of here?" Freddie was back, bustling in with her robe wrapped tightly around her. The color was high in her cheeks. Her mouth looked wonderfully well kissed. The sight made something inside Gabe twist hard.

"Gabe! I don't want to have to explain!" She looked desperate. And desperately unhappy, too.

Because he was going? Or because he hadn't gone last night?

Did she love him?

He didn't know. But even if she did...

"Gabe!"

"I know! I know!" He poked his head out. The coast was clear. He could hear Charlie and Emma both moving around now, but neither had appeared. He slipped downstairs.

His bags sat where he'd left them by the door.

He had only to walk across the room, pick them up and walk out. He could be out the door in five seconds flat. In his car in five more. There would be no more goodbyes. No more Charlie and Emma.

No more Freddie.

He shut his eyes. His fingers curled into fists. He didn't move.

Why not?

Because, damn it, it wasn't easy to ride off into the sunset when it was barely eight o'clock in the morning!

Footsteps clattered down the stairs. He turned to see both Charlie and Emma. Their eyes lit up when they saw him still there.

"Gabe!" They came hurtling down, only to stop dead when they spotted his bags still by the door. They stared at the bags, then looked back at Gabe. He gave a vague lift of his shoulders, then reached for his hat and clapped it on his head.

Emma sniffled. Charlie blinked rapidly.

"It was...pretty late by the time...I...reckoned I could just...leave this morning," he explained.

Behind them Freddie appeared. She was wearing a pair of jeans and a hunter green sweater. Neat and tidy. But her hair was still down—loose, flowing. The way it had been all night when he'd buried his face in it, wrapped his hands in it, rubbed his cheek against it.

He felt something lodge in his throat.

Freddie was stone silent, just looking at him. Her face was

pale. Pained. Not like the woman who had loved him last night. Like a woman whose heart was breaking.

Was it?

Was he walking out on her when she wanted him to stay? *Did* she want him to stay?

Staying meant marriage. It meant commitment. It meant responsibility. All the things that Gabe had been running away from for years.

It meant being like Randall.

Or…did it mean doing all those same things but in his own way?

"Can I come and see you, Gabe?" Charlie asked. "In Montana? Someday?"

"Charlie!" Freddie admonished.

But Charlie ignored her. His eyes were fastened on Gabe's. "Can I? Can I come an' learn to be a real cowboy? Someday?"

Someday.

Gabe thought about someday. He thought about all the somedays that would stretch out endlessly before him—with no Charlie, no Emma, no Freddie—if he walked out that door.

And suddenly, without thinking further, he blurted, "Why wait?"

"What?" Charlie and Emma and Freddie said together.

"Why wait?" he repeated. "Come with me. No time like the present." He spoke quickly, grabbing the notion, hanging on desperately, as if it were the rankest bull he'd ever rode. "I love you," he blurted. "You could marry me, Fred, and we could move to Montana. All of us. What do you say?"

The children's eyes lit up like Christmas trees.

Freddie looked poleaxed.

And Gabe, having reached the eight second mark of the scariest ride of his life, bailed. He couldn't wait and watch her reaction, couldn't face the judges' marks. He strode quickly out the door.

Freddie stared after him. Astonished. Disbelieving.

Hope sang inside her—and yet, shaking her head, she wondered if she had just imagined the whole thing. Had he said,

*I love you. You could marry me and come to Montana with
me?*

Had he said that—and then walked off?

Out by the car, Gabe, damn him, was whistling!

Desperate, she ran after him and grabbed his arm. "Look
at me."

He didn't. The color was high in his face as he shook her
off. He stowed his bags in the boot of the car. "I can't," he
muttered. "I'm sorry. I—"

And then she understood. Or dared to hope she did.

This was the way Gabe always was, whistling in the dark,
shaking in his boots whenever he really cared, determined, and
yet at the same time pretending it didn't matter.

She took hold of his arm again. "Gabe. I love you, too."

He stopped moving. But he still didn't speak.

"I know you're not Mark. And I know I'll be scared sometimes, but no more than you're scared now, Gabe. Please.
Look at me and ask me. Ask me again. I need you to. Please."

Slowly he turned to her. He looked at her long and hard
and deep—and gave her his heart in his eyes.

"I need you, too," he told her hoarsely. "You make me
want to commit, be responsible, do all those grown-up things
that Earl thinks will make a man of me."

"You're man enough already."

He grinned. And then he kissed her, long and hard and deep,
while Charlie and Emma danced and cheered. With a look he
shushed them, then turned back to her. "I love you, Fred.
Marry me? Come to Montana with me?"

Freddie touched his cheek, first with her hand, and then with
her lips. Then she slipped her arms around him and laid her
head against his heart.

"Yes, Gabe," she said. "Oh, yes."

* * * * *

Meanwhile, back at the ranch...
RANDALL

One

It was good to be back.

Randall came out of Bozeman Airport to the sight of snow. Last time he'd been in Montana, twelve years ago, it had been high summer, but now there was a magical beauty to the white-capped mountains all around the broad valley. He took a long, pleasurable breath. The air was like champagne.

He hadn't planned it this way. When Gabe set off for Devon to take charge of the *Buckworthy Gazette,* Randall had meant to visit some of the other Stanton publications, without, of course, telling Gabe and Earl. They could think he was resting.

As if!

If they thought he had time to rest, they knew nothing about Stanton Publications. Come to think of it, they did know nothing about Stanton Publications.

But it seemed they understood Randall. Earl's eyes had been opened to many things about his heir that he'd missed before—like that he was working himself to death. And Gabe's understanding of his cousin was instinctive. So the old man and the young had plotted to send Randall to Montana for a few weeks on the MBbar, while Gabe was in Devon.

He hadn't fought them very hard. His head had been aching, and a few weeks free from all cares had suddenly seemed very attractive.

"I'm going to be you for a while," Gabe had said, "so you can be me."

"Run the ranch?" Randall had queried, aghast. "No way, Gabe. I know my limits, even if you don't."

"Will you hush! It's January, the quietest month of the year. Anyway, my mom will be there. She'll do the stuff that needs a brain. You just relax and enjoy yourself with a bit of roping and riding."

Claire should be here to meet him, but there was no sign of her. At least, Randall didn't think so. She'd been twelve last time, and he might not recognize her now—not having noticed her much then, so to speak. She'd been a pest, forever trotting at Gabe's heels and scowling at him. That much he did remember.

Just when he was wondering if she'd forgotten him he noticed a tall young man in jeans, sheepskin jacket and a large hat, striding purposefully toward him. Closer inspection revealed the young man to be a young woman.

She positioned herself in front of him, thumbs in her belt, pushed back the brim of her hat and surveyed him critically.

"Lord Stanton?" She made it sound like a challenge.

"Randall."

"Claire. Sorry I'm late."

Randall took the hand she held out and nearly winced from the force of her grip.

"These yours?" She indicated his bags.

"Yes."

Randall reached down but she was before him, seizing the heaviest bag and moving off, tossing "This way" over her shoulder. He had no choice but to follow, carrying the smaller bag and feeling like a seven-stone weakling. He wondered if this alarming female would kick snow in his face.

She headed for a four-wheel drive pickup truck that had

seen better days, and tossed the heavy bag into the back. She would have seized the other if Randall hadn't firmly grabbed it.

"It'll take us an hour," she said, settling into the driver's seat. "You okay?"

"Fine, thank you. How is everyone? I'm looking forward to seeing Aunt Elaine again."

"'Fraid you can't," Claire said, swinging the vehicle out onto the Interstate. "She felt better, and wanted to see her Dad, so she went to London. You probably passed her mid-air."

"Went to—" Randall echoed in a hollow voice. His cherished picture of freedom took a knock. "You mean I've got to run the place?" he demanded, aghast.

"Don't worry," Claire said coolly. "Nobody's going to let you get your hands on anything important. We've got Frank, who's a great foreman. He and I will take care of things."

"I'm glad to hear it."

He was puzzled by her barely concealed hostility. Puzzled but not surprised. Claire had scowled at him when she was a kid, and she was still scowling at him, in a manner of speaking.

Claire was an orphan, raised on the ranch since she was a week old. She was devoted to the land, to her foster parents and above all to Gabe.

Randall glanced sideways, trying to get some idea of how she'd turned out. It was hard, even though she'd tossed her hat aside. Her hair was a rich dark red that might have been attractive if she hadn't scraped it back so that it lay against her skull with a kind of fierceness. Her skin had the pale porcelain look often found in redheads, and her eyes were a vivid blue. She might have been lovely if she hadn't seemed determined to squeeze every ounce of femininity out of her appearance.

"Have a good flight, Lord Stanton?" she asked.

"I'm not Lord Stanton," Randall explained. "That's my grandfather, the earl. I'm Lord Randall, but can't you forget that stuff and just called me Randall?"

''Not much point in being a lord then.''

''That's right.''

''Don't suppose you remember us much?''

''Well, twelve years is a long time, but I recall how lovely the scenery was. 'Course, that was summer.''

''You warm enough? I've got another sheepskin coat in the back.''

''Thank you, but I'm well provided.'' He added, slightly nettled, ''We do have winter in England, you know.''

''Not like a Montana winter,'' she said.

''All I know is that Gabe was bellyaching about the cold when I left.''

''How is Gabe?''

''Apart from the weather he seemed cheerful enough, certain he's going to knock their eyes out in Devon and show them all how to do it.''

She didn't answer. Her gaze was fixed on the road, for which Randall was grateful. It was lucky that the Interstate was almost empty, since Claire drove as though she owned every inch.

They were higher now, on the mountain pass, going east into Shields Valley. The great range rose around them, the air so clear that it seemed as if he could touch the peaks, although he knew they were far away.

Just as England was far away, he thought, and all the normal burdens of his life. And right now, that suited him fine. He leaned back in his seat with a sigh of pleasure.

Claire heard it and cast him a sideways glance of disapproval. Everything about him annoyed her, starting with the fact that he looked so much like his cousin. He had the same lofty figure, except that where Gabe was tall and rangy, Randall was tall and elegant. He also had hair of exactly the same shade of brown, plus lean, handsome features that were heartbreakingly like Gabe's.

Only he wasn't Gabe. And that was the worst crime of all.

This was the day Gabe should have come home, greeting her with a shout of welcome, smiling into her eyes, and then—

oh, please—then realising that she was the girl he'd loved all the time.

Instead she was stuck with this snooty English aristocrat, with his lofty air and his smooth voice, who thought he could just walk into the place. Run the ranch? Who did he think he was?

She knew she wasn't at her best just now. She ought to have managed a more convincing welcome. After all, it wasn't his fault that he wasn't Gabe.

Hell, yes it was!

"So what's my big brother up to?" she asked, trying to sound cheerfully casual. "Why's he staying in England? He told me something on the phone, but I couldn't make head nor tail of it."

Randall grinned. "He created a trap and walked into it himself."

"What does that mean?"

"He got worked up on my account, told the old man I was working too hard and I ought to take a break instead of going to Devon. Next thing, Earl challenged him to take my place, and it was too late for Gabe to back down. You know what he's like. Big mouth. Boy, is he in for a shock!"

In the pause that followed he was sure he could hear Claire grinding her teeth.

"Great," she said at last. "Just great. Did anyone—including Gabe—stop to think that he's needed here?"

"Does Gabe ever stop to think?" Randall riposted. "I remember last time I was here, he and I went a bit mad. Got ferried home by the sheriff more than once. It was always his ideas that landed us in trouble."

"That's right, blame him!"

"Blame?" Randall echoed hilariously. "You mean credit. He'd be mad as fire if he didn't get his due. Funny how women never seem to understand things like that."

He couldn't have said anything worse. Memories of that miserable summer flooded back to Claire: herself, twelve years old, hero-worshiping Gabe as she'd done since she was old enough to understand the world and her own place in it.

He was her savior, her idol, her god. Her childhood had been spent trotting after him, running his errands, happy when he talked to her, blissful if he deigned to spend time with her. And always dreaming that next year she would be old enough for him to notice her.

And then his cousin from England had come visiting, and immediately they had been as thick as thieves.

They'd spent all their time together doing things that excluded a twelve-year-old girl. Worst of all, they'd become "blood brothers," in what Randall, ignorant like all Englishmen, thought of as the traditional Indian manner.

One memory was especially sharp: overhearing Gabe say, "Don't tell that pest Claire about this. She'd only lecture us about 'Hollywood fantasies.'"

That night she'd cried herself to sleep. "That pest" was bad enough, but worse, far worse, was "Don't tell her—" Randall had gotten closer to Gabe than herself.

Now here he was again, keeping Gabe from her, sharing secrets with him, shutting her out. He'd been the enemy then and he was the enemy now.

Darkness was falling fast, causing the mountains to retreat into the gloom. Soon they were past and the plain stretched ahead. Without taking her eyes from the road, Claire said, "Gabe told me you were bringing something special—a gift to the ranch, he said, but he wouldn't tell me what."

"That's right. It's back there."

"Are you going to tell me?"

Randall hesitated. This wasn't the time or the place that he would have chosen. "Gabe was boasting about his herd of Herefords, so I started boasting about Rex. He's my prize Hereford bull, and what he hasn't won, isn't worth winning, and one thing led to another—" he paused delicately.

"Are you saying you've brought bull semen?" Claire demanded bluntly.

"Yes," he said, nettled. "Since you want to take the bull by the—er—horns, yes, it's bull semen."

"Why not just say so?"

"Well—a man hesitates to—I mean, with a lady he's only

just met, there are certain topics that—in polite company—
hell! Why didn't Gabe tell you?''

"Probably because he was having a good laugh imagining
this conversation."

"That sounds like Gabe."

"Anyway, no need to worry about polite company. You're
on the MBbar now."

They had just that minute passed through the wide gate with
the MBbar fixed over it, which meant three more miles until
they reached the house. At last it appeared, to Randall's relief,
for he was aching to stretch his long legs and get a warm
drink inside him.

The ranch house was a sprawling, two-story building, under
a light dusting of snow. Its center was one big room with a
polished wood floor, and brightly colored rugs here and there.
More rugs hung on the walls, and in the stone fireplace burned
a wood fire, its leaping flames reflected in the deep red leather
of the armchairs.

"Great," Randall said, looking around at the homely comfort with pleasure. "It's hardly changed, bar a few details,
from when I spent the best summer of my life here. Am I
sleeping in the same room?"

"You're in Gabe's room. His orders."

She made a dive for the large bag but Randall was too quick
for her, grabbing both cases and giving her a challenging look.
She returned it in full measure, so that he had a grandstand
view of the thrilling blue of her eyes, before leading him up
the broad wooden stairs.

When she'd left him Randall surveyed the bedroom with
reminiscent pleasure. This was where he and Gabe had slept
last time, yakking well into the night, reading forbidden books
by torchlight and sipping surreptitious slugs of whiskey. The
two beds had vanished, replaced by one large enough for a
big man to sprawl out on.

He thought of calling Gabe, then stopped as he realized it
was the early hours of the morning in England, although only
evening here. The long flight, plus the time difference, was

playing havoc with his inner clock. He yawned, trying not to be overcome by jet lag.

A shower in Gabe's bathroom made him feel better, then he searched Gabe's wardrobe and found a check shirt and jeans, which he put on. He'd brought very few clothes of his own because Gabe had told him to make free with his.

He yawned again and stretched out on the bed, feeling glad to be here. Other considerations aside, it would get him away from the "Hon Hon", as Gabe insisted on calling the Honorable Honoria.

The thought slipped in without warning and startled him. Only recently he'd half planned to marry Honoria. They weren't in love, but she was eminently suitable to be an earl's wife, and it was time he married.

Honoria thought so, too. At Earl's party she'd attached herself to Randall. People had called them "a lovely couple." And suddenly he felt trapped.

He wasn't sure what had changed, unless it was the effect of Gabe parachuting into his life without warning. That had always been Gabe's style—without warning. He was like a breath of fresh air; irresponsible, crazy Gabe, who never looked further than the next girl or the next slug of whiskey. It would be fun to "be" him for a while.

Imperceptibly, Randall ceased to fight off the jet lag.

Ten minutes later Claire knocked on his door, calling "Supper's ready."

Getting no answer, she looked in, and drew a sharp breath at what she saw.

The man who lay dead to the world on the bed wore Gabe's clothes, was the same lanky shape, and with his hair tousled from the shower, the likeness was emphasised. The sight struck Claire before she had time to arm herself against it, and suddenly her eyes blurred.

Moving quietly, she came closer. It might have been Gabe, and she could dream, couldn't she? Just for one little moment. She loved Gabe more than she could bear. He was so far away, and she was so lonely. She settled noiselessly into a chair and watched Randall, aching with some bittersweet emotion that was neither happiness nor misery, but an almost unbearable mixture of the two.

She didn't know that he'd awoken and was regarding her through his eyelashes, puzzled by her expression.

For her sake he grunted and stirred before opening his eyes fully, and that gave her time to get hastily to her feet and compose her face.

"I looked in to say supper's ready," she said gruffly. "I wasn't sure whether to wake you."

"That's very kind of you."

"No it's not," Claire said bluntly. "I'll wait for you downstairs." She vanished.

Randall pulled a wry face. Whatever Claire's virtues might be, they didn't include the social graces.

But social graces seemed to mean less than in his other life. What did matter was the long, pleasurable view of her he'd just enjoyed. Without the big sheepskin jacket Claire was revealed as slim and shapely, filling her jeans very nicely, thank you. Randall had swiftly revised his ideas. How could he ever have mistaken her for a man?

Gabe called her "my tomboy kid sister," and no wonder if she was so set on being one of the boys. But that was a pity. From his viewpoint she had a lot of potential for being one of the girls.

Going down a few moments later, he found Claire in the kitchen, stirring something in a pot from which were coming delicious smells. She'd released her hair and it was falling about her face, softening the fierce air that she wore like armor.

Randall held out his offering, a small, insulated unit containing Rex's finest. Claire received it without embarrassment and took it away to deposit somewhere safe. Randall looked around at the warm kitchen. In the center stood a large table, big enough to take ten, but laid for two.

"The others have had theirs," Claire explained, returning.

"The others?"

"North, Dave, Olly. They're all that's here now. In summer there'd be more."

While he waited, Randall looked around him, enjoying the sight of the old place again. Claire watched him with disapproval.

"It's not as grand as Stanton Abbey," she said.

Randall regarded her blankly. "Of course not. Nothing is."

Great! she thought crossly. This snooty Englishman was so lofty that she couldn't even needle him.

She ladled a thick stew onto two plates and set one before him. It was delicious.

As they ate he came to a sudden decision. "Mind telling me how I got on your wrong side?" he asked mildly. "There's an atmosphere you could cut with a knife."

"Gabe should be here attending to the ranch, not off on the other side of the world."

"But Gabe told me this was the quiet time."

"There is no quiet time," Claire said firmly. "There's a mountain of things to do."

"Then you'll just have to show me." He assumed a droll manner. "I'm a quick learner. I'm honest and tidy and—and I don't eat much," he finished triumphantly.

To his delight she gave a choke of laughter before she could bite it back. It lit up her face brilliantly, and he was fascinated. Then it was gone as though she'd slammed the shutters down, but Randall continued to regard her with pleasure.

"Why are you staring at me?" she demanded.

"I was wondering where you got that ravishing red hair."

"No idea. I was a foundling. Thought you knew."

"That's right, I did. Gabe found you in a box on the back porch when he was seven."

"Right. There was a note saying that someone called 'Abe Stevens' was my father. He was a hand that had worked here, but he was long gone by that time."

Randall grinned. "I remember Aunt Elaine saying how Gabe took you under his wing, acted like you were an unusual sort of puppy sent for him to play with."

Aunt Elaine had contacted the authorities, agreeing to care for the baby until the mother could be traced. But she never was.

"Gabe even chose my name," Claire said now. "And he badgered his Mom and Dad until they said I could stay."

Twenty-four years later she was still here. No wonder, Randall thought, that she was devoted to her "big brother."

"So nobody knows who I am," Claire said. "I could be descended from thieves, murderers—" She tossed the dubious possibilities at him defiantly, almost challenging him to say that she wasn't good enough to associate with a lord.

But she'd mistaken her man. Randall had met inverted snobbery before, and he knew how to deal with it. "Kings, queens, sultans," he supplied. "Your blood could be bluer than mine. And let me tell you something about blue blood. It doesn't start out that way."

"How do you mean?"

"The Stantons were some of the shadiest characters you ever saw. Gamblers, thieves, cutthroats, all of them low-life with an eye to the main chance. They made their money in various villainous ways, and when they had enough they bought their title and their big house, and pretended they were real aristocrats. Actually, of course, they were still as common as muck, but within a few years everyone who remembered that was dead. That was when their blood turned blue."

Claire gave another unwilling laugh. On the pretext of re-filling his plate, she studied Randall, not knowing what to make of him anymore. She wasn't used to men who talked like this. Gabe's humor was loud, up-front and boisterous. So, for that matter, was everyone's on the ranch. Even Aunt Elaine.

But Randall spoke with a quiet, fine honed irony; "British" humor, no doubt. It annoyed her to discover that she enjoyed it.

Randall looked up, grinning. "Don't let anyone fool you with that 'aristocrat' rubbish, Claire."

The grin was delightful. She looked away quickly. "Who's fooled?" she asked. "I saw through you at the start."

"I sure hope so."

He wished she would laugh again. It made a light come on

inside her, revealing things he wanted to know about. Why did she switch it off so fast?

"This food's good," he said. "Did you cook it?"

"It's just a stew."

"Best stew I ever tasted."

Instead of appreciating the compliment she rose and threw some more logs on the floor.

"It's been snowing on and off for the last few days," she said, "but I reckon tonight we'll have the big one."

She removed his plate and set another one, bearing a large piece of cherry pie, in front of him. Before he could stop her she scooped ice cream from a tub and dumped it on his plate.

"Hey!" he protested. "Are you trying to fatten me up?"

"Gabe eats ice cream like there's no tomorrow, and he never gets fat."

"But I'm not Gabe," Randall reminded her gently.

She set down the tub abruptly. "That's right." She removed the ice cream.

"Why don't you tell me about the mountain of things to do?" he invited.

"The big chore in winter is feeding the stock," she said. "They can't graze as they would in summer because the snow covers the grass, so we bring them in closer, to where we can keep an eye on them and take hay out to them every day."

Randall nodded. "I do the same with mine."

"You—personally?"

"No, I have stockmen. Does that matter?"

"I just wondered how used you were to turning out into the snow. You'll probably prefer to stay here and keep warm."

"No, I'd prefer to come with you," he said at once.

She was immediately conscience stricken. "Look, there's no need. I mean, just because I riled you—"

"You don't rile me, at least, not enough to make me do anything I don't want to do." He added wickedly, "But you can keep trying."

She was too wise to answer this directly.

"Tomorrow we'll take two trips, the first before breakfast."

"I'll go out with the second," he said. "I'm not a glutton for punishment.

"We go to bed early in winter," she said, "and get up at first light."

Randall yawned. "Suits me."

"Frank's away clinching a deal for Gabe at the moment. You'll meet the hands tomorrow." Claire hesitated. "You may not find them easy to get to know."

"I'll try not to let them intimidate me. Thanks for the warning."

They went upstairs together. In the corridor he said, "No need to escort me to my room. I'll try to remember the way."

"Fine. Goodnight." Claire opened the door to her own room, but stopped as if she remembered something. "You'll find some extra blankets in the closet. It gets real cold out here. Randall?"

He was staring over her shoulder at the little table by her bed. Claire followed his gaze, said a hasty "Goodnight" and shut the door.

Randall went on to his room, sunk in thought at what he'd seen. Right by Claire's bed was a photo of Gabe wearing his most wicked and appealing grin.

So that was it! Claire was carrying a torch for Gabe, and she was mad at Randall for being the wrong man.

Far from being offended, Randall found himself relaxing at being with a woman who wasn't out to catch him. After the perfect manners of Lady Honoria and other hopeful damsels, Claire's blunt disapproval came almost as a relief.

He was smiling as he climbed into bed, and asleep as soon as his head hit the pillow.

Two

Randall slept poorly because he had to keep getting up for more blankets. When it got cold in Montana, he realized, it really got cold. With every possible blanket on the bed, he was still barely warm.

At the first gleam of light he rose and sat by the window, swathed in blankets, to watch the dawn come up. It was magic: dark gray at first, then lightening to pearl as it crept over the huge, silent landscape of a Montana winter. Randall watched with a sense of wonder.

The estate attached to Stanton Abbey was large, but it had nothing like the eerie vastness of the MBbar. As first one building, then another took shape, Randall had a sense of ghosts coming out of the mist. From somewhere unseen a horse whinnied softly.

At last the land appeared, gleaming white, for Claire had been right about the snow. It had fallen heavily during the night and now lay thickly on the ground and against the doors.

Randall wasn't sentimental about snow, despite its beauty.

He knew it could be a treacherous enemy, and more so than ever in an exposed place like this.

But this morning he would have more than snow to worry about. He was about to meet the hands. And he had no illusions about how important it was.

Gabe had given him a brief rundown.

"Frank's the foreman. He and his wife have their own place on the ranch. He doesn't say a lot, but he's a great guy. There's only three hands at the moment, and they live in the bunkhouse."

He descended to find three men waiting for him, stamping their feet and blowing on their hands as though they'd just come in from the cold. Heads were raised as he came down the stairs. Eyes bored into him, watchful, sarcastic. It would have been unnerving if Randall had been easily unnerved.

The most prominent was a stocky, fair-haired individual in his thirties. He was handsome in a bullish, showy way, but he had a suspicious face. From Gabe's description Randall guessed that this was Dave, the chief hand. Beside him stood a man with a long white beard, and a head of thick, white hair, whom Randall knew was called Olly.

"As long as I've known him he's looked like the Oldest Living Inhabitant," Gabe had said. "So of course he became Olly."

Despite his white hair Randall noticed that Olly's cheeks were ruddy, and his eyes brilliant and lively.

The third man stood slightly apart. He was youngish, maybe thirty, tall and rangy, with dark hair and eyes, and a lean face. When the other two moved forward he stayed back.

Claire appeared and made the introductions.

"This is Dave," she said, indicating the stocky man who stretched his mouth in an unwelcoming smile. Randall felt his hand seized in a painful grip that he did his best to return with interest.

Olly's smile was friendly enough, but his grasp too was powerful. Afterward Randall resisted the temptation to flex his fingers.

"And this is North," Claire said, indicating the third man.

North kind of drifted forward and extended his hand vaguely, with an amiable smile. His handshake was firm without being a trial of strength. Of the three he seemed to be the only one without attitude, and Randall instinctively liked him.

Claire called, "Come and get it!" and the men converged on the kitchen.

Standing by the stove, stirring porridge, was a large, middle-aged Indian woman.

"Her name is Susan," Gabe had told him. "We took her on last summer to help cook for the hands. But when winter came and most of them drifted away, she had nowhere else to go. So she stayed."

And Randall had said, "Still collecting waifs and strays, I see." Gabe's casual kindness had always been the most endearing thing about him.

Claire was about to introduce him but Randall forestalled her, holding out his hand to the Indian woman and giving her his most charming smile.

"Hi, I'm Randall, and you must be Susan. Gabe told me all about you. He said you cooked the best gooseberry pie in all Montana."

She looked delighted but said nothing, showing her pleasure, instead, by heaping porridge into Randall's bowl until he had nearly twice as much as the others.

"You're going to need plenty inside you," Claire said, confirming Randall's thought that this was Susan's way of welcoming him.

He'd noticed that Dave took care to grab the seat beside Claire. As she moved about his eyes followed her.

Randall didn't blame him. Her face was prettily flushed from the stove, and the heat had made her hair float in soft wisps about her face. Randall regarded her, entranced, unaware that he was smiling at the picture she presented, until Claire noticed and frowned at him. He concentrated on his food.

Dave was eating fast.

"It's not going to run away, Dave," Claire told him, laughing.

"Sooner we're finished, sooner we get to work," Dave said flatly. "I'm still cold from the first time out."

He glared at Randall as though he was personally responsible.

"Last time I was here it was summer," Randall observed. "I'm looking forward to seeing the MBbar in winter."

He was making polite conversation, but it was the wrong thing to say, he knew that as soon as the words were out. Dave snorted his contempt.

"Snow ain't there for entertainment. It's there to make life hard. Guess you don't know that."

"We have snow in England," Randall said, refusing to be ruffled. "Just before I left I took some pictures of Gabe shovelling it away from Earl's front path."

"Earl?" they all chorused.

"My grandfather. We call him Earl because he's—an earl."

Their expressions told him he'd said the wrong thing again. But what was the right thing? Was there one?

"My grandfather was a miserable old sod," Dave observed. "But we didn't call him that. Leastways, not to his face."

"Perhaps you should," Randall said at once. "It might have improved him."

North gave a snort of laughter. Olly grinned. Dave scowled. North said, "Thought earls had servants to clear their paths."

"He does," Randall confirmed. "But he said since he had a pair of lazy lummoxes for grandsons, they could make themselves useful." Hoping to lighten the atmosphere, he added, "I'll get the pictures."

Once out of sight upstairs he leaned back against the wall and let out a long breath. This was going to be tougher than he'd thought. Well, at least it would make life interesting.

He found the photographs and headed back downstairs. As he descended he heard the sound of laughter, followed by Claire's voice, reproving but on the verge of a chuckle.

"Cut it out, Dave. He's not that bad."

Dave's donkey bray of laughter made Randall wince. He stayed where he was, shamelessly eavesdropping.

"Not that bad?" Dave roared. "He's the best entertainment we've had around here in months. Did you feel his hands? Not a callus anywhere."

"He's a lord," Claire observed. "They don't have calluses."

"Then he sure came to the wrong place," Dave observed.

"He won't last here," Olly said. "Fifty dollars says he's on the first plane out tomorrow."

"You don't have fifty dollars," North observed mildly.

"No sweat. I won't need it."

"Give him a chance." That was Claire.

"Sure we'll give him a chance," Dave said. "A chance to ride Nailer." He brayed again.

"No way," North broke in, his mild voice sounding unexpectedly firm. "Claire, you can't let him ride Nailer. Not until you know if he can ride."

"All aristocrats can ride," Claire said. "But you're right. I don't want to have to explain to Gabe how his cousin got a broken neck."

"That Gabe!" Olly chuckled. "Trust him to think of a joke like this. Boy he must be laughing!"

"Did you hear his voice?" Dave chortled. "Did you hear his *voice?*"

He seemed totally overcome with mirth, which turned into a coughing fit. There was the sound of hands slapping a back, as if the rest were trying to stop Dave from choking to death.

"Don't try too hard, folks," Randall murmured.

He stayed sunk in thought for a moment. By the time he went down the rest of the stairs he'd come to a decision. If that was how they wanted to play—Fine!

He returned to the table, seemingly unaware of how the talk stopped at the sight of him. He laid the pictures down with an air of lofty indifference. Dave grunted, but the others spread them out with interest.

"Who's Santa Claus?" North asked, pointing to a gleeful, red-cheeked figure.

"That's my grandfather, Lord Cedric, Earl Stanton, Vis-

count Desborough, Baron Stornaway and Ellesmere, heredi-
tary lord of the manor of Bainwick," Randall said coolly.

"Don't look like an earl," Olly observed.

"That is not necessary," Randall observed in his most dis-
dainful voice. "What matters is to possess the lineage, and to
have people know that you possess it, eh? What?"

That would show them, he thought. If they expected him to
talk as though he was chewing nettles, then that's what he'd
do. Eh? What?

Claire was frowning at him as though wondering why he'd
suddenly started to talk the kind of English normally heard
only in bad stage productions. He was going to wink at her
and share the joke, but North claimed his attention, and when
he looked back she'd returned to the kitchen to get bacon and
eggs.

"Sleep well?" she asked him when she returned.

"Excellently!" he said in a robust voice. "Except for being
rather too hot. But after I threw off a couple of blankets I was
fine." He saw the others staring at him, and said blandly, "We
learned to be hardy at Eton, dontcha know?"

"You'll need to be hardy out here," Dave said. "Can you
ride?"

"Dave!" Claire muttered in an undervoice of protest. "I
told you—"

"I was in the army, old bean," Randall declared in a bored
voice. "In the Household Cavalry. Guardin' the Queen."

Dave looked about to be overcome with mirth again, but a
glance from Claire kept him quiet. Susan went around refilling
coffee cups, doing Randall's first, and the moment passed.

At last they all got up from the table. Randall went upstairs.
North and Olly went to the bunkhouse. Dave stayed behind
muttering to Claire.

"Even Susan's all over him because he's a lord."

"It's not that," Claire said. "I think it's because he spoke
to her so nicely. Some people act like she's part of the fur-
niture."

She turned a significant eye on Dave, who was the chief
offender. He grunted and quickly moved off. Claire had to

admit that she'd been impressed by the way Randall had put himself out to be pleasant to Susan.

Just like Gabe, she thought quickly. In fact, Gabe probably advised him to do it.

Susan bustled in to clear the table, casting an appreciative eye on Randall's empty plate. "What a nice boy."

"Of course, he's Gabe's cousin," Claire reminded her.

"He's more handsome than Gabe," Susan said slyly.

Claire bristled. "He is not."

Susan chuckled and withdrew under a mountain of plates. Claire looked around, then reached into her shirt where she'd hidden the picture of Gabe that she'd secreted from the pack. Susan's switch of allegiance gave a new poignancy to the face that laughed back at her from so many thousand miles away.

Randall, coming downstairs a moment later to retrieve the photographs, stopped, held by the sight that met his eyes.

Claire was standing there, regarding Gabe's picture with a look more piteous than words. For once her face was soft, defenseless, and Randall felt as though he'd had a blow to the heart.

Poor Claire, he thought. What a rotten thing to happen to her, being landed with me. I shouldn't have come.

Randall wasn't more sensitive than the next man, or especially in tune with the feelings of women, as several ex-girlfriends could have testified. But something about Claire's dumb anguish got under his radar, and reached his heart before he knew it.

He'd never felt this kind of empathy for anyone. She was almost alone in a household of men. His Aunt Elaine, though a kindly soul, had a robust attitude to life that might make her hard to confide in. From what he recalled of Martha, she was much the same. Besides, she wasn't around now. Claire was isolated, trying to be one of the boys while coping with a woman's feelings, knowing them unrequited.

She was rough, awkward, bristly. But she was also unhappy and lonely, and his heart went out to her.

She moved and he quickly retreated back up the stairs. It

would be fatal for her to find him intruding on her private sadness.

In his room he finished getting dressed, and was about to leave when an impulse made him turn back and pick up the phone by his bed. It would be late afternoon in England, and Gabe ought to be ready to take calls.

"May as well see if he ever managed to find the place," Randall muttered with a grin. Slightly to his surprise Gabe was not only there but he answered the phone with a terse "What now?"

Randall stared at the phone. That was never his happy-go-lucky cousin, surely. He sounded as if the pressure had gotten to him already.

"Gabe?" he responded cautiously. "How's it going, then? Are you all right?"

It was amazing how Gabe's voice changed when he knew he was talking to Randall. "Of course I'm all right," he said too quickly. "What do you think?"

"I just…thought you might need a little moral support," Randall said cautiously.

"Well, I don't. I'm fine. No problem," Gabe said airily.

Randall ground his teeth. Trust Gabe to use his charm and get all the locals dancing to his tune on the first day.

"Nothing to worry about," Gabe went on. "A child could do it."

I'll bet that's meant as a dig at me, Randall thought.

"How are things at your end?" Gabe asked.

"Fine," Randall declared, imitating Gabe's airy tone. "Couldn't be better."

Couldn't be better, he thought, except that Claire hates me for not being you, and the hands crease up every time I open my mouth, and the only one who doesn't wish me dead is Susan.

He hung up with Gabe's parting injunction, "Don't call me again," ringing in his ears. He wondered if Gabe could tell he'd been lying through his teeth.

Come to that, how much truth had Gabe been telling? He'd probably been lying, too.

The thought made Randall feel suddenly better. It might be uncharitable, but at least he wasn't suffering alone. He was grinning as he picked up his jacket and headed for the door.

He opened it to find Claire standing there. "I came to see if you'd dressed up right," she said.

"Gabe's thickest shirt, old bean." He held out his arms in display, and she came right into the room.

"What are you wearing underneath?" she asked.

"I beg your pardon?"

She began to unbutton his shirt. For a moment Randall thought his wildest dreams were about to come true, but her brisk manner dispelled his hopes. She took his undershirt between her fingers, testing to see how many thicknesses she could find.

"You're only wearing one undershirt," she accused him.

"My dear gel, that's winter long johns. Gabe warned me. And it's cashmere, the warmest wool in the world."

"Put two more on top of it. You want pneumonia? Socks cashmere as well?"

"The very finest."

"Three pairs. You'll need 'em."

"You wouldn't care to undress me and put them on, I suppose?" he asked. "I forgot to bring my nanny with me."

"So I see." She hesitated and added, as if reluctantly, "Be careful about Dave. Don't get him mad."

"I'm a big boy, Claire. I survived in the army. I think I'll survive the hands." He added wryly, "Whether I'll survive you is another matter."

"Is that an example of British humor?" she asked suspiciously.

"No, it's called black humor. It's for when your neck's on the line."

She was too cautious to answer this directly. "Hurry up. We want to be setting off."

She departed in a whirlwind.

"Yes, ma'am!" Randall murmured, beginning to strip off.

As he worked he ground his teeth, annoyed with Gabe, annoyed with Claire but mostly annoyed with himself. The feel of her fingers unbuttoning his shirt had caused a flare in his loins that he would have denied if he could.

But he couldn't. He tried to dismiss it: a knee-jerk reaction, inevitable when a woman opened your shirt, because your subconscious was remembering other occasions. Nothing at all if you looked at it rationally. But it had been there, a swift spurt of pleasure, fierce, hot and totally crazy. He was wearing long johns, for pete's sake. And so was she, probably. Three pairs. Old men's underwear.

But how would she look without it?

He pulled himself together and tried to think pure thoughts. But the memory of Claire's womanly shape got in the way and the thoughts took on a life of their own.

Thank goodness it was freezing cold outside, he thought desperately. It needed to be.

When he'd added several extra layers of clothes he went down.

Monk, the horse they'd given him, was big and lively, but he'd handled tougher beasts in the Household Cavalry, and he and Jackson soon came to an understanding.

A white moonscape stretched before them as far as the eye could see. Beyond it were the mountains. The sun was brilliant on the snow. But the cold was bitter, and he silently gave thanks to Claire for making him put on the extra clothing. When he saw her glancing at him in mischievous enquiry he grinned and gave her a thumbs-up salute. Dave watched them through narrowed eyes.

Four gigantic horses stood ready, harnessed to a huge sled full of hay. A signal from Dave and they were off, over the silent landscape, now brilliant in the sun.

Randall began to enjoy himself almost at once. The Stantons had been landowners for centuries, and he was a countryman born and bred. Years spent in offices, staring at figures, seemed to fall away from him as he rode out that morning.

The haystacks were huge, and the hay had to be forked off them by sheer human effort. It was back-breaking work, but it reminded him how enjoyable it could be to feel his body

alive with effort, the blood pounding through his veins as
though he'd just come back to life after a long sleep.

The cattle knew why they were there, and crowded forward
eagerly. Randall remembered his own cattle, his in the sense
that he owned them, but in no other sense. Other men and
women fed and tended them, knew them. Until this moment,
he hadn't felt that as a deprivation. Now he knew it was.

Sentimental nonsense! he tried to tell himself. But the
thought wouldn't go away.

On the way home Jackson made one last effort to be the
boss. Randall gave him his head, controlling him lightly, enjoying the gallop. Then he heard hooves pounding beside him
and realized that Claire was drawing level, making a race of
it. He grinned and urged Jackson on.

Out of the corner of his eye he managed to watch Claire,
controlling her enormous horse with confidence and grace, her
eyes alight with purpose. Nothing fazed her, he realized with
admiration.

He thought of Honoria, who insisted on riding only well-
mannered horses, and would turn back halfway through the
day because she'd broken a fingernail. Randall, who enjoyed
a robust ride in the country, had found it irksome.

Suddenly Claire's horse stumbled on some unseen obstacle
in the snow. Alarmed, it reared up. Claire fought for control,
but she'd been taken by surprise, and she fell to the ground,
landing on her back with a crash that made Randall wince in
sympathy.

"Claire!" he cried and turned back.

"I'm all right," she yelled. "Get my horse."

He seized the bridle so that she could let go and concentrate
on scrambling to her feet. She wasn't all right, he could see
that. She moved like someone who was hurt and determined
not to show it. But he guessed that any show of sympathy
would madden her.

She remounted, patting the horse to show there were no
hard feelings.

"I'm surprised you could get up at all," Randall said.

She tried to shrug, and had to give up the attempt. "It's nothing."

The others caught up with them, and Dave pushed ahead to ride at Claire's side. All the way back his voice was raised in a dreary recital about something or other. Randall didn't bother listening to the words. His attention was for Claire, who was drooping slightly in her saddle.

He longed to push Dave aside and tell her she could lean on him. But he knew better than to try.

Three

Getting into bed that night Randall moved very, very carefully. He enjoyed an active life, but the day's exertions had used muscles he wasn't familiar with, and he ached all over.

At last he gave up the struggle to find a comfortable position and hauled himself painfully out of bed. Somewhere in this place they must keep some liniment. Preferably lots of it. He should have asked before he came upstairs, but he wouldn't give them the satisfaction.

Easing on his dressing gown he crept out into the corridor, wondering where was the best place to look. But as he made his way past Claire's room he realized he'd reached the end of his search. The smell of liniment came unmistakably from behind her door.

Now he could hear painful little gasps, reminding him of how she'd fallen onto her back. She was trying to get to places she couldn't reach, and it was hurting her.

He tapped softly. "Claire."

The door opened a crack. Claire stood there, wrapped in a large towel.

"I'm looking for the liniment." He gave her a friendly smile. "Some instinct made me look here."

"I've just finished with it."

"Are you sure? You must be bruised all over your back. Can't I help—as one sufferer to another?" When she still hesitated he added, "I won't tell if you won't."

That won him a faint smile. "Sure." She backed away to let him in, holding defiantly onto the towel.

He didn't look around the room too obviously, but he noticed that the picture of Gabe had been removed from her bedside. She was protecting herself.

She sat down with her back to him, and he gently loosened the towel, drawing in his breath at what he saw.

"You've got the biggest bruise I've ever seen," he exclaimed.

"Bet some of yours are bigger," she said bravely.

"Bet they aren't. Lie down, let me do this properly." He saw her reluctance and said, "To hell with modesty! You're going to be fit for nothing in the morning."

"I feel fit for nothing now," she sighed, stretching out on the bed.

He eased the towel down the length of her back, waiting for her to rally her defenses and tell him to stop right there. But she seemed too worn out to speak and he began gently rubbing liniment into her skin.

It was lovely skin, he couldn't help noticing, pale and smooth. After her brusque mannerisms it came as a slight shock to find her body so softly rounded and feminine.

He began to wonder if he'd been wise to do this. Even with the ugly discoloration of the bruise, she was beautiful. Her back was long and elegant, tapering to a tiny waist and hips that flared into round, womanly curves.

He moved his hands rhythmically up and down her spine, trying not to hurt her. Trying even harder not to be too aware of her. But that was impossible.

"This will make you feel better," he murmured. "What would we do without liniment, eh?"

"Well, we wouldn't smell like horses, that's for sure," she said with a yawn.

"Yes, it's a pity about the smell."

If she were a horse, she would be a racehorse, he decided: with a proud, high-stepping beauty and a flowing red mane. Her hair had come loose and splayed over her shoulders. He pushed it aside and began kneading the back of her neck. She gave a little grunt of contentment that went straight to his heart, making him smile.

"Is that nice?"

"Mmm," she said.

She raised an arm to pull her hair right out of the way, then rested her head on her elbow. He guessed she was growing too hazy to realize how the movement made the towel slip, and drew one glorious breast into view.

He forced his eyes away from the tantalizing sight, wondering what had possessed him to take such a risk. But the boyish clothes she wore had disguised the details that were designed to tempt a man. Now he realized that her breasts were heavy in proportion to the rest of her. In fact each one was just about the right size to fit into the palm of his hand.

He tried to force his thoughts away, but they were more rebellious than his eyes. They insisted on wandering over what he could see of her body, and even creeping under the towel to discover hidden secrets. He knew he should be ashamed, fight down the heat that was surging through his body, taking over from good resolutions. He drew a long breath, trying to subdue himself, but the part that was reacting most vigorously wasn't amenable to thoughts.

"It wasn't such a bad day," he said, talking for the sake of it. "Bit rough, but I was expecting that."

"Mmm!" she said.

"I'll manage better now. Practice makes perfect and all that." He had an uncomfortable feeling that he was burbling, saying anything, trying to hear the words through the roaring in his ears.

Get out before you do something that will make her slap your face!

"What's the program for tomorrow?" he asked, smoothing his hands down to her waist and forcing himself to stop there. "Claire? Claire?"

Her breathing had deepened, telling him she was asleep. He froze, his hand still on her waist, shocked at himself. This had begun so innocently, but now his whole body was aroused. Claire rejected feminine wiles but without trying she was simply the sexiest woman he'd ever known.

But she was also the most vulnerable, especially now.

That's how much you inspire her, he thought. *You send her to sleep. Get out of here.*

While he hesitated Claire gave a long sigh and moved very slightly, so that her skin slid against his hand, making his fingers drift involuntarily lower.

Involuntarily? Who was he trying to kid?

She settled down again, making a little contented sound in her throat, smiling a small secret smile.

For Gabe! he thought suddenly. She was dreaming that this was Gabe. If she awoke and found him there her sense of betrayal would be terrible.

Breathing hard, Randall rose to his feet and backed away. He found he was actually shaking from the force of the sensations that possessed him. He must put things right before there was a disaster.

But there was something he must do first. Moving carefully, not to awaken her, he pulled up the towel until it covered her again. Then he took the sheet and blankets that she'd pushed down, and inched them back into place, so that she would be kept warm.

When he was finished he backed out of the room and stood in the corridor, taking deep breaths.

It was only then that he remembered he'd left the liniment on her bedside table. He cursed but there was no help for it. Hell would freeze over before he risked going back in there.

He returned to his own cold, solitary bed and lay down to spend the rest of the night struggling with the pain of bruises and frustrated desire.

*   *   *

Randall was late coming down the next day. He'd finally
fallen into a late doze and slept on. Susan explained that Claire
had ordered that he shouldn't be disturbed. The others had
already gone out to work.

There was some sausage and bacon left. He would have
been happy with it, but Susan insisted on cooking him a huge
meal from scratch, and he didn't have the heart to hurt her
feelings.

Afterward he called Gabe. He'd been too easily put off by
bright pleasantries the day before. They needed a serious talk.

But all he got was a young woman informing him that,
"Mr. McBride is in conference with the advertising editor and
does not wish to be disturbed."

"But that doesn't mean me. Tell him it's Randall. I can
give him a few wrinkles about advertising."

There was a click and some muttering, then the secretary
announced, "Mr. McBride thanks you for your call, but is
unavailable."

Randall breathed hard. What the hell did she mean, "Mr.
McBride"? This was ol' Gabe they were talking about. Wasn't
it?

"Then kindly give 'Mr. McBride' a message," he said.
"Tell him to stop playing the fool and come to the phone."

More clicks and muttering. Then, "Mr. McBride says he
will call you back."

"Tell him to do that," Randall said, incensed.

He was left staring at the receiver, wondering what sort of
idiot game Gabe thought he was playing. He needed Randall's
help and advice, and he was damned well going to get it—
just as soon as he answered the phone.

Looking around the house, he discovered a computer, and
switched it on. As he'd expected, Gabe had treated himself to
all the latest software.

"Are you any good with that thing?"

He turned to find Claire looking at him. Her face was neu-
tral and there was nothing to be learned from it.

"Reasonably," he said.

"Elaine does the accounts," she said, "but I promised to

keep them up-to-date while she's gone." She left the implication hanging in the air.

"I'm a dab hand with a spreadsheet."

Luckily it was a program he knew. Claire showed him some invoices waiting to be entered, and soon he had the hang of Elaine's system.

The hands began to drift in, full of amusement at his defection.

"Guess one day's hard work was enough for you?" Dave said gleefully.

Randall shrugged, refusing to be provoked. "I was late getting to sleep," he said.

Claire had avoided looking at him directly, but at this he sensed her whole body come alive. She was standing next to him and he was convinced, as surely as if he'd touched her, that the memory of last night was there in her flesh as well as her mind.

She knew what had happened as well as if he'd said the words, knew he'd lain awake most of the night, tormented by her. The awareness was like an erotic vibration coming from her, catching him up in its rhythm. It would have told him everything, even if he hadn't been able to see the delicate pink come and go in her cheeks.

"I guess you'd just about had enough," Dave chortled.

"Leave it, Dave," Claire said quietly.

"Aw, c'mon—"

"I said leave it!"

The fierceness in her voice was like a burst from a flamethrower. All the hands fell silent, astounded by an intensity they'd never seen in her before. They began to drift off, until Claire was alone with Randall.

"I'll see Susan about some food," she muttered and hurried into the kitchen.

Coward! Claire told herself furiously. *Coward! Coward!*

But she hadn't wanted to be alone with Randall after that moment of revelation. She hadn't wanted to see him this morning either, not after the hectic dreams that had tormented her last night. Dreams in which his hands were always on her body, touching her intimately as no man had ever touched her before. And she'd offered herself shamelessly to his caresses.

He'd been lucky to have lain awake, for the wakeful could control their thoughts. They didn't return to consciousness burning with shame at the way desire had overcome them while they were helpless.

She'd told Susan to let him sleep because she couldn't face him. That was the truth. He would be bound to look at her and know that she'd taken his brotherly help and wrought it into something else.

When she'd found him at the computer she'd felt relief. They could act normally, as though the moment had never happened. But she hadn't allowed for the mutual consciousness that had possessed them, destroying her carefully built defenses.

And then there was Gabe, whom she loved, but whose image had never tormented her like this. He didn't want her passion, so why did she feel as though she'd betrayed him?

In the days that followed Claire was careful never to be alone with Randall. Luckily North seemed willing to take him under his wing. Dave, who fancied himself as a wit, had taken a marked dislike to Randall, and had a stream of barbed remarks always at the ready.

Randall countered this by becoming more and more British. Nothing Dave said ever seemed to get under his skin. He would merely look at the hand from under languid eyelids, smile insufferably, and murmur, "I say, old bean—no really—"

It reduced North and Olly to fits, and it drove Dave wild.

Once Randall had casually mentioned that Gabe had taught him to use a rope. Dave had promptly challenged him to a contest and Randall had agreed before she could stop him.

"Dave's the best for miles," she told Randall urgently. "There's no way you're going to beat him."

Randall had given her that strange look from under his eyelids and murmured, "There's more than one way to skin a cat."

At first she thought this was just bravado. Randall's roping skills could hardly be described as skills at all. What had possessed him to put them on display?

Dave's mouth was twisted into a mean little smile, and he gave his braying laugh. "Guess it ain't like being in the Household Cavalry," he said gleefully.

"I'll just have to practice," Randall said meekly. "Let's try again."

He whirled the loop high and wide and it floated down to settle perfectly over Dave's shoulders, pinioning his upper arms.

"Hey!"

"I say, I'm most awfully sorry. I'll have it off you in just a jiffy." Randall tugged at the line, apparently overcome by confusion.

"You're just pulling it tighter," Dave bawled.

"Oh dear, yes I am—if you'll only keep still—"

"Let me go, you idiot!"

There were more snickers, but this time at Dave's expense. Olly chortled openly, North grinned and Claire made choking noises.

At last Dave was freed. He glared malevolently at Randall. "You did that on purpose," he raged. "You made a fool outa me."

"My dear fellow, I wouldn't try to improve on nature."

"You—"

"Cut it out, both of you," Claire said, barely smothering her laughter. "Come in and have something to eat."

Luckily, Frank arrived just then, back from an errand in town, and in the introductions the moment passed.

But it wasn't forgotten. Randall guessed that Dave could be a bad enemy, and he would have to watch his back.

Claire was beginning to realize that there was more than one type of man. There was the kind she'd always known out here, brash, up-front, rawly macho. And there was the kind who deflected an enemy with cool irony, endured quietly, but never yielded an inch, the kind whose apparent mildness covered steel. Randall's kind.

He was a gentleman. Before this she'd never defined the word for herself, but the night he'd seen her half-naked might never have been for all the use he made of it. There were no sly hints, no attempts to make her uncomfortable with the memory. It was a delicacy of feeling that would have made the others hoot with derision, had they known.

But they didn't know, and must never know. It would remain their secret, hers and Randall's.

The discovery that they shared a secret alarmed her. It was a step toward an intimacy she didn't want. She was very firm in her own mind about that.

But then, being human and contrary, she began to wonder if Randall's gentlemanly restraint actually covered indifference. From there it was a short step to feeling offended. How dare he act as though it hadn't happened!

She caught herself watching him. She tried not to, but her eyes refused to be controlled. They persisted in drifting toward him when they should have been elsewhere. They noted every inch of his big, graceful body, the outline of his thigh muscles against his jeans, the thickness of his neck and heavy shoulder muscles, the suggestion of power in his most careless movement.

That evening she came into the kitchen and found Randall helping Susan with the washing up she understood something else about him. He didn't need to trumpet his masculinity because everything about him was so unmistakably male that his confidence came from deep within. The others could laugh if they liked. He would merely shrug.

"Go to bed, you must be tired," she told Susan, gently edging her away from the sink and taking her place.

And Susan went like a lamb, concealing her smile. She knew what was what without needing it spelled out.

There were still plenty of dishes to wash, and in handing them to Randall to be dried Claire found their fingers touching more often than not. She could have simply placed the plates in the rack, but this didn't seem to occur to her.

"You must be tired too," Randall said gently. "You run

this place, do a share of the housework and still come out working with us every day.''

"Trying to get me to stay at home?" she asked at once.

"Hey, don't be so prickly. How about changing the routine and showing me some of the district?"

She concentrated on the sink. "North can show you. I'll give him the day off."

"I rather think Gabe would expect you to do the honors."

Trapped, she thought dizzily. Forced to spend a day alone with him. She bent over the sink lest her happiness show in her face.

Next day they set out in the truck, headed for the little town of Marmot where Claire needed to pick up some supplies.

Marmot consisted of Main Street and little else. There was a drug store, a post office, a grocery, a meat locker, a hardware store and welding shop, an implement dealer, a few bars, a cafe, and a place that sold one of everything because that was all there was room for. Randall, accustomed to tiny English villages, was instantly at home.

The weather had improved. Snow still lay on the ground, but the sun was out and everywhere had a bright and cheerful appearance.

They went from store to store, collecting goods and introducing Randall. Everywhere there was the little start of amazement as people saw his face. When everything was loaded onto the truck Randall said casually, "I think I'll let you treat me to a coffee."

They found a little place, and she bought them both coffee and pie. When they were seated he realized how little he'd seen of her. This was the first time they'd been alone since the night he tended her, and he wondered if she was avoiding him.

How much did she remember from that night, and how did she remember it? In his fever of longing had he done something unforgivable?

She looked up quickly, met his eye and looked away. A soft, pink blush glowed in her cheeks, and the conviction grew on Randall that whatever he'd done it hadn't been unforgivable.

A middle-aged man, called Joe, hovered, wanting to know if everything was okay. It was the third time he'd done this, so Randall lifted his head to give the man a good view of his face.

"That better?" he asked amiably, and Joe grinned.

"You gotta take him to the dance," he told Claire. "Folk'll just blow their minds."

"What dance?" Randall asked.

"There's one here every February," Claire told him. "Just a few folk."

"They come for miles," Joe assured him. "And they'll sure come to see him."

"I seem to be the local entertainment," Randall observed wryly. "Mustn't disappoint them, so we'd better go to this dance."

"We?"

"I can't go alone. I shall need you to hold my hand and give me courage."

"You don't mean half the things you say," Claire told him lightly. "I've learned that much."

He didn't answer in words, but raised one eyebrow quizzically. Suddenly she burst out laughing. It utterly transformed her face. Her eyes glowed, her cheeks were still rosy from the cold wind outside and for a moment she seemed the very essence of youth and life. Randall felt giddy. Gabe could have this fantastic, beautiful girl, and didn't want her? Was he nuts?

"What are you laughing at?" he asked.

"You, raising one eyebrow. Do you remember when you were here before, Gabe envied you because you could do that? He could only manage both at once."

"That's right," he said, remembering. "We had a contest."

"I caught him practicing in front of the mirror, but he couldn't manage it. He got so mad."

She laughed again, and Randall joined in for the sheer pleasure of sharing it with her.

"The things that seem important when you're eighteen," he mused.

"Would you want to be eighteen again, Randall?" she asked.

He thought for a moment before shaking his head. "I guess not. I'm not sure why. I was happy enough then, the way boys are happy, without thinking."

"And aren't you happy now?" The question came out before she could stop it.

He might have made some meaningless answer, but he found himself thinking, then answering honestly.

"Fairly. Nobody ever gets back that carefree feeling, but you don't need it. You grow into a different person and other things start to matter."

"You don't mean that, about becoming a different person."

"When I look back so far, I hardly recognize myself. Do you?"

"Yes," she said with a touch of defiance. "But I guess I'm not changeable."

He spotted the danger and stepped back from it quickly. Damn Gabe! Why did he have to get in everywhere?

"Let's get going while the light's still good," he said.

She took the road up into the mountains. It was the way they'd come the first day, but then they'd been in semi-darkness. Now he could look around him and appreciate the glowing blue, white and black of the earth and sky.

"Stop here," he said when they were at the highest point before the road began to slope down.

He got out and went to survey the magnificence around him. Claire came to stand beside him.

"If you look far over there, you can just about make out the ranch," she said.

It was cold after the heated truck. He felt her shiver and put an arm around her. In the same moment he felt the sky and the mountains begin to whirl around him. He closed his eyes and took a deep breath.

She held onto him. "The mountains affect some people like this."

"Yes," he said, opening his eyes.

"Randall, are you all right?" She touched his cheek lightly with her fingertips.

He took her hand in his and looked at it for a moment before drawing it against his mouth, and letting his lips brush against it lightly.

He hadn't meant to do it—at least, he didn't think he'd meant to—but he was still giddy, and not quite sure what he was doing. And then, suddenly, it was done, and he was aflame from the sweet touch of her hand on his mouth.

She was trembling in his arms and for a moment, standing on the edge of the snowy vastness, he could have done anything. Her lips were softly curved. Just looking at them drove him to madness, and in another moment they would be against his own—moving softly, enticing him, opening for him.

"Randall…" she whispered.

"Yes," he muttered thickly.

"We—shouldn't stand here in this wind—it's dangerous."

A tremor went through him. "You're right," he said at last, reluctantly. "We should be going home. It's very dangerous here."

Four

___

Where did the time go? One day he arrived at the MBbar, the next he went out with the hands, feeding stock, coming back aching all over. And then he fell into the rhythm of the work and the life of the ranch, so that it became not easy, but possible. A week slipped away, then two, and suddenly he'd been there a month.

Bit by bit he began to enjoy himself. In England he was subject to Earl's endless demands that the business make more and more money. However long the hours he worked, he never felt he could satisfy the old man.

But here nobody expected anything of him. Or rather, they expected the worst, and there was pleasure in showing that he was as good a man as any of them, could fork hay as long and vigorously as they could, survive the cold, ask for no quarter. In Montana, Randall was finding his own level, not as the heir to an earldom, but as a man among men. It was a high level that gave him pride in himself.

And friendship. When had he last had time for that?

There was time now to make friends with Frank, a man he instinctively respected. Time to let Olly teach him to cheat at cards. Not that he would use that particular skill, but he appreciated the honor.

The friend he valued most was North. The young cowboy sought him out, asking questions about England and other countries Randall had visited, and listening avidly to the answers.

"Where do you come from?" Randall asked him once.

"Up north."

"Hence the name? I mean, it's not your real name?"

"Is now."

Another time North observed, "Reckon you and me are alike. Neither one of us care what folks think."

"Don't I care?"

"Wouldn't put on that dang fool voice if you did."

"True."

"Ain't usin' it now. Must have forgotten."

"No use putting it on with you," Randall pointed out. "You don't fall for it."

North merely grinned.

Randall began to be aware of the land. Though it was still hidden under the snow he found he'd developed a feel for it, almost as though it were his own.

Many a day he would rise and watch the dawn, when the world glowed pink and purple under the morning moon. And in the late afternoon he would slip out alone to see the sunset. The unbelievable beauty of the snow with the red and yellow light on it took his breath away.

Sometimes Claire would come and stand beside him, and they would watch together in silence. Once she asked, "Is it as lovely as this in England?"

"Yes," he said. "But softer, more pastel colored."

"Do you miss it?"

He thought of the pearly light over the corn, the gentle rustle of the stream he'd fished as a boy, the willow bowing its head into the water.

"Yes," he said. "I miss it."

And for once he wasn't alive to her reaction, and didn't see the look she gave him.

Another time, when the last light had almost gone, and a breathless hush lay on the land, Randall almost found the words to speak of the feelings that were growing in him, for her. But she spoke first, looking up into the sky.

"What do you think Gabe is doing now?" she whispered.

And his words died, unspoken.

His body, too long trapped behind a desk, grew iron hard under the rigors of winter work. He began to fill out, but it was muscle, not fat. There was a vibrancy about his flesh that made him alive to new sensations as he hadn't been for years. And the sensation that plagued him most was his growing desire for Claire.

He'd wanted women before, but seldom felt such pressing desire for one he couldn't have. The rare women who refused were casually asked and soon forgotten. But Claire was different. She mattered. Because she mattered, he minded that he couldn't have her. And because he couldn't have her, she mattered more than ever.

She enchanted him as no woman ever had. He loved—that is, he was attracted by—her defiant courage and her flashes of vulnerability. He was entranced at the way she tried not to find his British humor funny, and the little gurgle she gave when she was defeated. But what made his head spin with total delight was the feeling that something was about to happen between them. He didn't know what, or when. But it was going to be momentous.

One night Randall was awoken by a sound downstairs. He listened and it came again, a kind of scratching. Pulling on jeans and a shirt he made his way along the corridor and halfway down the stairs to where he could see the big main room, lit by only one table lamp, beside the leather sofa.

North was by the bookshelf, going from book to book, studying titles with such fierce concentration that he didn't hear Randall. At last he found what he was looking for, pulled

it out and went to stretch out on the sofa. He glanced up as
Randall came down the rest of the way.

"Mrs. McBride don't mind me looking at her books," he
explained. "She says nobody else ever does."

Randall collected the whiskey bottle and a couple of glasses.
"Charles Dickens," he said, observing the spine. *"Great Ex-
pectations."*

"Began on him when I came here last summer. Goin'
through, book by book."

Randall was startled. In all his time at Eton and Oxford he'd
never come across anyone who read their way right through
the collected works of Dickens even for study, let alone for
pleasure. He put a glass of whiskey by North's elbow, and
settled himself comfortably in a leather armchair. The fire had
burned low but it was still pleasantly warm.

North jabbed at the book. "I tell you, this guy knew how
to tell a story. That Miss Havisham, she was just like my Aunt
Nell. Ol' Nellie took a shine to this fellow, had the weddin'
all set, then he rolled in the hay with her cousin."

"Did she live in her wedding dress for twenty years?"

"Nope, but she threatened and cussed every man she saw
after that. Kept a shotgun in the corner, 'case a man showed
his face."

Randall eyed him, fascinated. "How long will it take you
to get right through Dickens?" he asked.

"Maybe until next summer," North said. "Then I'll go.
Don't like to hang around."

They sipped their whiskey in companionable silence. Randall leaned back in the armchair and studied the ceiling.

"You really gonna ride Nailer tomorrow?" North asked
after awhile.

"Guess so."

Another long silence.

"You're a fool," North observed.

"Must be."

"Know why he's called Nailer?"

"Probably for something I'd rather not know about."

"'Cause he's a brute who'll 'nail ya' if he can."

"Reckoned it was something like that."

"Wouldn't ride him if I was you."

"Yes, you would," Randall said with conviction.

North considered this. "Guess I would at that," he said at last. "But then I'm used to him. I know he throws to the left, so you gotta lean to the right."

"Then won't he start leaning to the right?"

"Nope, 'cause he's stupid. Mean and stupid. And he likes to get you off in the first two seconds, 'fore you can settle. If he doesn't manage that it gets him good 'n' mad."

"But do I want to get him good 'n' mad?" Randall asked plaintively. "I'm shaking with fear as it is."

"Yep, I noticed that," North said with a grin.

"So what else can you tell me about Nailer?"

"Well, he—" North stopped and a cunning look came over his lean, amiable features. "Make a deal?"

"Anything you like."

"No kiddin'. There's something I want real bad."

"Anything in my power."

"But no telling the others, right?"

"It'll be just between us," Randall assured him, growing more mystified by the minute.

"'Cause they wouldn't understand, and I don't want folks thinkin' I'm strange."

Randall tore his hair. "North, will you just tell me?"

The young cowboy put up a callused hand to scratch his forehead. In the firelight his face looked like teak. He leaned closer to Randall like a conspirator.

"Can you get me some Jane Austen?"

Next morning Randall logged onto the internet, found an online book store and bought a complete set of Jane Austen, using his own credit card. He grinned as he thought how Dave and Olly would react to its arrival. "British wimp" would be the kindest thing they'd call him. But he would keep North's secret. He owed him that much after all he'd learned the night before. Jane Austen had come up trumps in a big way.

Claire came in just as he was logging off.

"Why are they bringing Nailer out into the yard?" she demanded, aghast. "Don't tell me you're fool enough—"

"Fool enough for anything," he confirmed.

"You don't know what you're doing. I'm putting a stop to this."

Randall rose quickly and grabbed her arm as she made for the door. "You'll do no such thing," he said, assuming his most lordly "British" air. "My dear gel, I've committed myself, and the Stantons never back down from a challenge."

"But you'll break your neck."

He lifted his chin. "Then I shall go down with honor!"

"Will you stop talking like that, you—you *aristocrat!*"

"Is that the worst you can find to call me?"

"For the moment, yes, but I'm working on it."

"Try 'toffee-nosed git'," he teased.

"Dammit all!" Claire breathed. "Can't I ever say anything that you mind about?"

Randall's eyes held a curious alert expression. "That would hurt me, you mean?" he asked.

"No, I—of course I don't—what do you think I—"

He touched her cheek with a gentle finger. "If you want to break my heart," he said quietly, "you could do it far more easily than that."

He strode off without waiting for her reply. Claire looked after him. Her pulse was racing and she was suddenly breathless.

Full of shame, she realized that she had been trying to hurt him. She'd been trying to do that ever since he arrived, punishing him for not being Gabe. Punishing Gabe.

But Gabe was far away from her thoughts right now. All she could hear was the soft drawl of Randall's voice as he said—what? What had he really meant by those mysterious words about breaking his heart?

Who cared about Randall's heart? Her own heart belonged to Gabe.

But she couldn't resist touching her cheek, which seemed to burn where he'd caressed it. Then she hurried out after him.

The hands were waiting in the corral. Dave and Olly sat

gleefully on the fence, Frank lounged against it, while North held Nailer's reins. The huge brute stood still and silent, but Randall wasn't fooled. This was one mean horse.

"Don't forget everything I told you," North murmured, so softly that only Randall could hear.

He nodded, took a deep breath and vaulted up into the saddle.

"Let him go."

North complied and stepped back hastily. The next moment Randall felt as if the earth had heaved him off. He landed back in the saddle with a crash, just remembering to lean to the right. He gripped with his knees, but Nailer bucked violently again and sent him back up.

On the second landing, he tensed his knees faster and managed not to be thrown up so high the next time. Nailer bucked and bucked, always unseating him a little, but not enough to get him right off. And, as North had predicted, he was getting good 'n' mad at not succeeding at once.

Then Randall made his mistake. Allowing himself a small feeling of triumph he lost concentration, and suddenly he was flying through the air, to crash into the ground with a force that nearly knocked the breath out of his body. He gasped violently, and fought for control, forcing himself up before he was ready. Anything rather than let them see he was winded.

His head was spinning but he managed to get to his feet. North had gotten hold of Nailer who was standing still again, apparently calm except for the heavy snorts that were coming from his nostrils. There was an evil glint in his eye, as though he was eager for another bout.

"He beat ya!" Dave chortled, getting down from the fence.

"The hell with that! I'm getting back on."

"Look, we know you can't make it—"

"Get out of my way!"

Something in Randall's voice made Dave back off. As Randall vaulted back into the saddle North grinned and released the rein just in time to escape Nailer's whirling hooves.

Now it felt like a battle to the death, with no quarter asked or given on either side.

Whenever Randall went down Nailer came up, colliding with him so hard that he wondered why his bones didn't shatter to fragments. He gritted his teeth and hung on. Slowly, agonizingly he was getting into Nailer's rhythm, and at last he could instinctively throw his weight into the right position for clinging on.

Despite the cold, the sweat was pouring down his face, into his eyes. Every part of him was aching. In fact he was hurting so much that he could no longer feel it. A twist of Nailer's body brought Claire into sight. He had a brief glimpse of her with her hands pressed to her mouth, her eyes wide, before Nailer twisted again, and he lost sight of her. He must stay on. There was no way he was giving up in front of Claire.

It was stalemate. The horse couldn't get rid of him, but he wasn't tiring. Randall began to feel desperate. For some reason winning this battle was the most important thing in the world right now.

Nailer's violent movements brought him back within Claire's range. And now he wondered if the ordeal was making him hallucinate, for he could almost have sworn that she was cheering him on. She vanished from sight too fast for him to be sure.

On and on it went until Randall thought it would never end. Just when he felt he was about to black out, Nailer came up with his final trick. He gave in, not slowing gradually but stopping so suddenly that Randall nearly went over his head. He clung on, wondering what had happened to the world that seemed to have reversed and started spinning in the opposite direction. When his head cleared he realized that he'd won.

North and Olly were dancing with glee, filling the air with ear-splitting shrieks. Dave glared. Claire had buried her face in her hands, but as Randall sat there, brushing the sweat out of his eyes, heaving like a set of bellows and feeling as if his body was about to fall apart, she lifted her head.

Her eyes were shining. She was all aglow with some inner radiance that was for him. An answering light came on inside Randall. Had any man ever been looked at like that before?

It took all the strength he had left to get off Nailer without collapsing. The ground swayed again as his feet touched it, but North was there to steady him. He would have taken charge of Nailer, but Randall tossed the reins to Dave.

"Put him away for me, old thing," he requested languidly, and walked away toward the house. He would have liked to adopt a nonchalant saunter, but his lower half was completely numb and it was as much as he could do to stay upright.

He heard the sound of footsteps behind him, and then Claire was at his side. Without a word she drew his arm about her shoulders, and felt him lean hard on her.

"I never thought you'd do it," she said, exhilarated.

As soon as the door closed behind them he staged a mock collapse. Laughing, she put both arms about him and helped him to a chair.

"I'll get something for your head," she said.

"Uh-uh!" He was too wrapped up in the feel of her arms around his body to concentrate on her words. He felt light-headed.

She helped him off with his shirt and undershirt, exclaimed over his discolored body, and fetched a bowl of water. Randall became aware that blood was trickling down his face.

"That was a nasty fall you took," she murmured as she sponged him. "You'd better see the doctor, fast."

"No way. I shall eat my breakfast and then come out to work."

"You'll do no such thing. Do you realize nobody has ever ridden Nailer first time before? Even Gabe had to give up the first time. 'Course, he was younger then," she added quickly.

"Of course," Randall said, entranced by her nearness and her fresh, flowery smell.

"There's a good doctor in town," she went on. "I'll drive you in."

"Claire, I can't do that," he said seriously. "I've got to carry on as normal, just like the others would. Surely you can see why?"

"But you might have cracked a rib," she pleaded. "Or worse."

"I don't think so." He felt his rib cage carefully. "Seems OK to me. See what you think."

She set the sponge down and began to feel him gently. She'd treated enough broken bones on the ranch to know at once that he was right. But her hands didn't know how to let him go. They lingered on the thickness of his torso, taking far longer than they needed to.

There was a light dusting of hair over his chest—she'd wondered about that. His muscles were as firm as any cowhand's, and his skin was warm.

He was still heaving from his exertions, and Claire felt the movement of his rib cage against her fingers. She wanted to go on exploring, and the desire shocked her.

"You—don't seem to have any damage," she said at last.

"Not to my ribs," he said.

He spoke so quietly that she wasn't sure she'd heard right. She looked up quickly to find him regarding her with a look that made her suddenly aware how strongly her heart was beating.

Reluctantly, she let him go. She was full of confusion and nothing made sense anymore. She dabbed at his head again, but distractedly, and there was a distant look in her eyes.

"No blue blood," Randall joked. "It's the same color as yours."

She gave a brief smile. "I was a pain, wasn't I?"

"Just a little prejudiced at first. I guess I understand that."

"No you don't," she said quickly. "It was just—well, never mind. I'm not used to strangers."

"How long can a man be a stranger?" he asked.

"Guess you haven't been a stranger for a while now," she said quietly.

How soft her mouth was, he thought, when she dropped her guard. How badly he wanted to kiss it! In another moment he would throw caution to the wind, lean forward, and it would happen. He drew a sharp breath. His pulses were racing. It was a long time since the mere prospect of a woman's kiss had filled him with such anticipation. In fact, he couldn't remember when he'd last had to tread so carefully. The girls at home were only too eager to attract Lord Randall's interest.

"Claire—"

She turned on him a defenseless smile that destroyed his resolve. She was too easily hurt. Everything mattered so much to her. He couldn't kiss her, knowing he would go away in a few weeks.

"Yes?" she asked.

"Nothing," he said reluctantly. "Can you give me a hand up the stairs?"

"You want me to rub some liniment in your bruises?"

"Most of them are in a place I'd better see to myself," he said wryly, and felt his heart lurch at the sound of her chuckle.

That night they had a celebration. Frank arrived with his wife and grown daughter. Susan outdid herself with the cooking, the hands cheered Randall—at least, North and Olly did— and Claire produced some of Gabe's best wine.

During the day Randall had come to a decision about Claire. His growing attraction to her was threatening to get out of control, and he had to fight it. Not for his own sake, for hers. Only recently he might have regarded her armored heart as a challenge, but he'd seen how easily she could be hurt and it had altered him. Nothing in the world looked quite the same anymore. Time to call a halt, before it was too late.

There was nobody to warn him that when a man started saying things like that, it was already too late. But when he saw Claire come down actually wearing a dress, he knew his good resolution was going to be harder than he'd reckoned.

It was a simple, old-fashioned dress, made of flowered cotton, with a fitted waist and a slightly flared skirt. Randall's fashionable lady friends would have screamed with laughter.

But he didn't feel like laughing. He was too busy catching his breath at the sight of the sexiest woman he'd ever seen. He'd already known that Claire had long legs. Now he discovered that she had slender ankles and shapely calves, and when she moved her hips the dress fluttered this way and that, whispering promises.

She'd brushed her glorious red hair until it shone, and caught it back lightly in a loose, twisted braid. She was like a pre-Raphaelite goddess, risen from the earth, smelling of spice and honey, arms outstretched to the sun.

Randall caught himself up on the thought. He'd never been a fanciful man, and this was a helluva time to start.

With two extra women the evening turned into an impromptu dance. Someone put a tape on, and Randall danced with Frank's wife and daughter. And after that, of course, it was his plain duty to dance with Claire. She was his hostess and it would have been rude not to.

He tried to be strong. Remembering his resolve, he waited until the music turned lively, and everyone "danced" by bouncing around, doing whatever they liked. He held her hand while she twirled, and felt her brush against him, and each time it was like an electric shock.

But suddenly the music changed to a sweet waltz, and then no power on earth could have stopped him taking her in his arms. When he felt the softness of her slim form against his, he knew he'd been waiting for this moment forever, and no amount of good resolutions would be any use.

Despite her boyish ways she was as light and feminine as a fairy in his arms, moving softly and with an instinctive grace that enticed him to fit his movements to hers.

Wasn't dancing supposed to be a substitute for making love? If so, it was a very poor substitute. He was achingly aware of her body beneath the clothes that he would have liked to strip away. Were her breasts really as heavy and beautiful as he recalled from that one glimpse? And would he ever discover the truth?

He knew he was holding her too close, or was it that she was pressing herself against him? Looking into her eyes, he found them fixed on him, hazy with wonder. He smiled, and when she smiled back it felt as though she was kissing him, opening the sweet, womanly mouth that tantalized him and…

The music stopped. Claire sighed, looking as if she'd just come out of a trance. Randall released her before they could attract attention, but when she slipped away to the kitchen he followed her. She was stacking dishes, moving as though only half aware what she was doing. He drew her firmly away from the sink and into his arms. His mouth found hers and locked onto it as though his life depended on it.

For a moment he felt her hesitate, as though her mind was resisting what her flesh wanted. Then she relaxed against him.

She was as sweet as honey, and as heady as wine. He might never have kissed a woman before, so different was this one. If only the others in there would go to perdition and leave him alone with her, to do what he'd been wanting to do since the first moment.

His tongue found the inside of her mouth, felt her accept him eagerly. Her body was pressed against him and he was intensely aware of her shape. But it wasn't enough. He wanted more, all of her, everywhere his hands could reach.

It was exactly ten hours, thirty-five minutes and twenty seconds since Randall had vowed never to do this. Now it might have been another life.

A shout from the big room warned him that someone was about to come in.

"Damn," he said unsteadily. "Claire…"

"Hush, let me go," she pleaded.

"Later—"

She didn't have a chance to answer. Suddenly the kitchen was full of people.

Surrounding Claire, bearing her away, leaving Randall wondering how much more of this he could stand.

Five

When the party was over and she was alone, Claire put on a heavy coat and slipped out of the kitchen into the snow, hoping the freezing air would calm her down.

Nothing made any sense. The conviction that had sustained her for years—that no man in the world could mean more to her than Gabe—was tottering. It was as though some mighty power had taken her life by the scruff of the neck and shaken it, and her, until everything was a new shape.

She wasn't sure about the new shape. Nothing about it was familiar. But oh, it was sweet, with a poignant sweetness she hadn't experienced since the year she discovered she was in love with Gabe, and known it was only a matter of time before he loved her back.

Only he never had. And now she knew he never would.

She'd tried to believe that Gabe's brotherly affection was inching toward the kind of love she wanted from him. When he'd tired of the others he would come home to her. That was what she'd told herself.

But her first experience of true passion in Randall's arms had blown that illusion away, leaving her stranded in a vacuum, not knowing what lay behind or before her. Not knowing what she wanted. But Randall had whispered, "Later..." and she had replied, "Yes."

If they'd been alone in the house she knew what would have happened next. It was as inevitable as night following day, but only because they both wanted it.

Now it really was night. Randall had gone up to his room, and he would be waiting for the sound of her foot on the stairs.

"Thinks he's pretty clever, doesn't he?"

She jumped. Dave was standing there, evidently having just come out from the bunkhouse. He moved nearer to her and she could see, as well as hear, his bitterness.

"The great English lord?" he sneered. "Passing the time with the local wenches. That's what they call it over there, ain't it?"

"Shut up, Dave!" she said firmly. "You know nothing about him."

"Aw, c'mon. We all had him sized up from the start."

"You had him sized up as a wimp," she reminded him. "But he rode Nailer the first time. Took you three goes."

"Any fool can ride a horse."

"But Randall's no fool," she said quietly.

"Right!" Dave seized on this. "He's got that lordly estate to keep up, and he's got to marry a girl with blue blood. What color's yours, Claire?"

She turned bitter, burning eyes on him, and Dave took a hasty step back in the snow. Who would have thought Claire could look like that over any man?

"I'm just talking as your friend," he said, trying to regain lost ground. "I'd hate to see you hurt. 'Sides, I thought it was ol' Gabe you were sweet on—"

"Stop it!" Claire said, speaking so fiercely that Randall, standing at his window just above, heard her and pushed the window open. Looking out into the chill night he heard her say, "Don't ever dare speak to me about Gabe."

"Hell, you know how I feel about you, Claire—thought maybe it could be my turn. I've waited long enough."

At the window above, Randall tensed at the sounds of a scuffle, as though Dave's lust had overcome his manners. Looking down he could just make out the two figures struggling outside the kitchen door, and hear Claire mutter, "Get off me!"

The next moment Randall was out of his room and tearing down the stairs, racing to the rescue of his lady.

But he made it only as far as the kitchen. Even from outside he could hear the sound of a sharp slap, and Dave's yelp of pain and surprise. Then Dave staggered into the kitchen. Randall had a brief glimpse of him clutching his face, before he backed away into the main room, hoping Dave hadn't seen him in the darkness.

Standing there, unknown to either of them, he grinned at his own folly in thinking of Claire as a damsel in distress who needed his help. What a right hook she must have! What a girl!

Claire's voice grew clearer, as though she'd followed Dave inside. "You get out of here right now," she raged. "And don't ever come smarming around me again."

"Hell, I'm sorry," Dave mumbled. "I just thought—"

"No, you didn't," she said crossly. "You don't know how. All you can do is jump to conclusions. Get this straight. I'm in no danger from Randall. Maybe he is just passing the time, and maybe so am I. Lord knows, he looks enough like Gabe!"

"You mean—"

"Yes, I do. It's always been Gabe for me, and it always will be. I'm telling you that to get rid of your stupid ideas, and if you repeat it to a living soul I'll box your ears so hard your head won't stop ringing for a week. Now get out."

When Dave had scuttled away to the bunkhouse Claire shut the outer kitchen door firmly behind him. She was shaking, and on the verge of tears, but she refused to cry.

Dave's words about Randall had struck home so painfully that she'd said the first thing she thought of to put him off the scent, not knowing whether it was true or not.

She'd always loved Gabe. But it was the memory of Randall's lips on hers that made the fierce heat start up inside her. Gabe had never kissed her, never looked at her with the ardor she'd seen in Randall's eyes. Perhaps if he had...

Oh, she couldn't think of Gabe right now. He seemed so far away, not just in distance, but as though he was no more than a vaguely remembered dream. It was Randall who mattered, Randall who was here now, whose kisses sent her mindless with need, and who was waiting for her upstairs now...

As she stood in the darkness, trembling with the force of her emotions, she thought she heard a sound from the next room, but when she went in and switched on the light, there was nobody there.

Because he was no saint, but a very human man, Randall's reaction to the news that Claire's heart still belonged to Gabe contained as much pique and annoyance as pain.

She'd been teasing him. And after his good resolutions about her! Not that they had amounted to much. But for what he'd overheard he knew he would have taken Claire to his bed and made love to her until they were both exhausted. The thought of it made him ache still.

The next day, Claire didn't mention the fact that he hadn't gone to her room that night, and nor did he. He could hardly tell her that he'd heard what she said to Dave. She was probably relieved that he hadn't showed up.

The one he was really mad at was Gabe, who'd gotten in the way just when he wasn't wanted.

He called his cousin on his bedroom phone, and reached him easily enough. But Gabe bent his ear with a long description of Freddie Crossman and her children. Randall liked the Crossman family but he hadn't thought there was so much to be said about them. He wondered if Gabe knew that he said Freddie every second word.

He came off the phone, thoughtful.

Downstairs he found Claire struggling with the computer.

"I've just called Gabe," he said, when he'd finished sorting out her problem.

"Oh, yes. Has he bankrupted you yet?" she asked cheerfully.

"If he has, he was careful not to mention it." A thought struck him. "I'm not sure I really care. It all seems a long way away. It'll feel strange to go back."

"Did Gabe mention when he was coming home?"

"No, we never got around to that." He was suddenly reluctant to pursue that subject.

"He can't leave it too long," Claire said. "It'll be spring soon, and that's when the real work starts."

"What we've been doing isn't real work?" Randall asked plaintively.

"You think this is work? Just wait until we start calving. Then it's up at all hours, checking, fretting, delivering calves when the mammas can't do it on their own. We're always exhausted. But there's nothing like it. Nothing like being there when a newborn calf takes its first breath, when you've made a difference, when—" She checked herself. "Of course, you won't be here, will you?"

"No," he said abruptly.

Then, because he couldn't think what to say next, he went away.

That became the pattern over the next few days. They would talk about something that seemed safe. Then one of them would stumble and bring the conversation to an abrupt end. She never asked him why he hadn't come to her room that night, and he never broached the subject. Everything between them was unresolved, and likely to remain so forever, as the day of his departure neared.

Strangely, it was easier to communicate when they were not alone. He discovered that when she came in late one evening, when he was talking to North about the MBbar.

"I understand now why Gabe once told me he couldn't live anywhere else," Randall was saying. "I feel that way about my own land."

"Yours? Thought you were just the heir," North said.

"I am, but I rent one of my grandfather's farms. I hardly

see it because I'm chasing newspapers all the time, but I keep promising myself I'll go back to farming for good.''

"Why don't you?" Claire asked, pouring them both whiskey, and settling down on the floor, by the fire.

"Well, I can hardly let the old man down. His publishing empire means so much to him. So I let it drift, promising myself, next year, and next year.''

He sighed, looking into the drink.

"Now I feel like a man who found the right woman, deserted her, then found he'd made a mistake.''

The words hung between them. North looked from one to the other, but Claire's eyes were on the fire, not Randall.

"It's easy to make some kinds of mistakes," she said.

"And some you spend your life paying for," Randall agreed quietly. "It can be hard to know what you really want, and sometimes you only find out when it's too late. And you think—if you'd done something sooner—''

"But maybe you can't," Claire interrupted. "We don't really have any say, do we? Things happen, and we react, but it's never really up to us. It's like someone's pulling the strings and having a good laugh.''

"Hell, Claire," North said in alarm. "You're a philosopher.''

She laughed shakily. "Nobody ever called me that before.''

"Philosophy doesn't solve any problems," Randall said. "Only feelings do that.''

It seemed a good moment for North to slip away, leaving them alone. And he did. But when he'd gone, Claire said awkwardly, "Well, I suppose it's about time to be turning in.''

"Yes, it must be. Goodnight, Claire.''

"Goodnight, Randall.''

That's how it was between them these days.

On the night of the dance Randall presented himself downstairs, hoping he looked right.

North was there, sunk deep in Jane Austen, which he'd carefully covered in brown paper. He jumped, but relaxed when he saw it was only Randall. Randall grinned.

North eyed the soft flannel plaid shirt. "That'll do."

"It's Gabe's."

"I know. Claire gave it to him last birthday."

"Oh, lord!" But before Randall could go up to change it Claire appeared on the stairs and both men turned, dumbstruck.

She'd swapped the flowered cotton for an olive-green silk that followed the lines of her figure with flattering emphasis. North indulged in a long, fervent wolf whistle.

"Claire, when you buy a new dress, you sure buy a new dress!" he exclaimed.

"It's not new," Claire said quickly. "I've had it over a year."

North frowned. "Could have sworn I saw it in that catalogue you got two weeks back, and—"

"You've got shaving cream on your cheek," she interrupted him.

It wouldn't do to let Randall suspect how she'd pored over the pages of that catalogue, trying to find just the dress that he might admire: how she'd paid an extra charge to be sure it arrived on time, how she'd agonized in case it didn't fit.

But it had got there in good time, the fit was perfect and Randall was smiling at her in a way that made her tremble.

"You look beautiful, Claire," he said softly. "Really beautiful."

"Do I look like those fashionable ladies you know back home?" she couldn't resist asking.

"Not a bit," he replied. "Thank goodness."

The late February dance was the big event in the locality, a kind of promise that spring wasn't far away. Everybody went, including Susan, and there wasn't a vehicle left on the MBbar.

Frank called with his family, to collect Dave. North drove Susan and Olly in an old sedan that was kept for emergencies. Randall and Claire went in the truck.

"What's that book North keeps hiding under the cushions?" she asked when they were out on the road.

"Leave a man his secrets," Randall said with a grin.

"But it's in a brown wrapper. North isn't reading porn, is he?"

At this Randall shouted with laughter.

"What is it?" she demanded. "Randall, what is it?"

"I can't tell you—I promised—" He went off into another paroxysm of mirth, and the next second he'd lost control of the truck.

For a few hairy moments they spun on the icy road. He heard Claire gasp, and he prayed frantically, wrestling with the wheel. But it was more luck than driving that brought them to rest against a tree with a jolt that sent her sprawling against him.

"Claire?" he said in fear. "Are you all right?" His arms were tight about her.

"I'm fine," she said. "What's a little bump?"

He clasped her more firmly. "I thought we were both goners then."

"Mmm." She knew she should move, but it was so comfortable here in his arms, and instead of releasing herself, she rested her head on Randall's shoulders.

"Claire?"

"Mmm?"

"Do you really want to go to this dance?"

"No," she said dreamily. "I don't."

"Neither do I."

They sat in silence for some moments, letting the alarm of the moment before die down, just enjoying themselves.

"Shall we go back?" he said, so softly that he wondered if she heard him. She didn't answer in words, but she lifted her head, and nodded.

They drove back in silence. The house, too, was silent when they reached it, and growing chilly as the fire burned low. Randall piled on some logs and the flames flickered up, throwing dancing shadows over Claire's face, for they hadn't put the lights on.

Randall put his arms right around her and drew her close.

"Claire," he said thickly. "Claire, I—"

"Don't talk," she whispered. "We've both said too much, and it only makes problems."

"But are you sure—?"

"Hush," she silenced him with the touch of her mouth.

They kissed feverishly, but it was only a brief prelude to what was to come. They both knew now that they couldn't stop at kissing. The feeling of their mouths in contact only increased the need to touch each other everywhere.

They chose her room, the place where he had first seen her half-naked, first wanted her with a crazy longing that had given him no peace ever since. It had been physical then. Just physical. Wanting to touch the soft hills and valleys of her contours, wanting to caress her intimately, to claim and conquer.

But somewhere along the line it had become more. When had it begun to be so important to win her stubborn, contrary heart? And would he win it like this?

He would know in the morning. But that was a long way off.

The lovely dress, so carefully chosen, slipped to the floor. Claire barely noticed. It had done all she asked of it. Every inch of her was fevered with longing. She must have him, and soon. Only the feel of his body united with hers could ease the ache of need that had been growing in her for weeks. She wanted to touch him everywhere, with her hands, her lips, her breasts, her thighs.

At some point Randall had removed his shirt, and when he drew her against him and she felt the silky hair of his chest, it excited her still more.

His hands moved up until he could cup her breasts in his palms, letting his thumbs drift slowly across their fullness again and again. The sensation was so good that Claire drew a long shuddering breath. Her nipples were peaked and hard with anticipation, and the pleasure radiated out from the rasping movements.

She was aware of his body tensed against hers, the stomach hard and flat, the thighs steely with power. Her heart skipped a beat as she thought of that power. He was her first man, but she was no ignorant girl. The sheer force of her feelings for

Randall had taught her what it was like to be caught up in desire, possessed by it, altered beyond recognition by it.

His lips burned her shoulders and she let out a long breath. Randall heard it and thought he understood.

"Claire—do you want me?" he murmured.

"Yes—" she said raggedly. She could hardly speak the word for the roaring in her ears.

"Let me hear you say it," he commanded.

"I want you—"

She wasn't sure whether she'd said the words aloud, for her whole body seemed to be saying them in its clamorous response. She wanted him. She wanted him now.

Her arms seemed to find their way about his neck of their own accord, and she was kissing him frantically, trying to drive him on to the thing she craved with all her being.

"Randall," she whispered, "Randall—"

Some new note he heard in her voice seemed to decide him. He began to toss aside the rest of his clothes, and she quickly did the same. When they were both free he drew her down onto the bed. After his earlier urgency he seemed content now to take his time, enjoying her with his eyes and his hands.

He rested his face between her breasts, pressing his mouth against the silky skin, bestowing light kisses and exploring until his lips touched one proud nipple and began to tease it. She thought she would go out of her mind with that sensation. Her breath came in long, slow gasps that shaded into groans, and she wove her fingers in his hair, pleading, yearning, demanding.

His response was to insert his knee between her legs which fell apart for him. She gasped as she felt his movements become more purposeful.

Slowly, with a fierce, controlled power, he entered her. As she felt him drive in deeply Claire knew that this had been inevitable from the first moment, and that it was right. She arched against him, wanting more. He was triumphant, but so was she as they did the thing for which they'd both been born. She held him close, wrapping her thighs about him, imprisoning him for her delight.

He watched her out of dark brooding eyes, her hair spread out over the pillow, her face wild with ecstasy. Her soft moans of pleasure excited him further. "Claire—"

His thrusts became deeper, harder. All his power was now concentrated on being one with her. She was lost to everything but this, driving back against him in mindless delirium, asking and giving. They were two halves of a whole, perfectly attuned to each other, finding completion together. The moment, when it came, was shattering, a long, ecstatic climax in mounting waves of pleasure that peaked and crashed, fading away and leaving them trembling. Claire cried out and clung to him, hearing his voice in her ear, saying her name over and over.

As they parted he held her more tightly than ever, not wanting the moment to pass. And she clung to him, as though she needed him to hold her hand to the end of the journey. Randall knew she'd given him what she'd offered no other man. Gabe might have been her first love, but he'd been too dumb to value her. So she'd turned to Randall, who did, pouring out lavish gifts of beauty and passion that awed and humbled him. He wondered if she had any regrets, but soon she propped herself up on her elbow and looked down at him.

It was too dark to make out her expression, but he could see a faint glint in her eye, and hear her soft chuckle.

"What are you laughing at?" he asked in delight.

"Nothing. I'm just happy."

He pulled her down, feeling her long hair flow over him like a river.

"Be happy, Claire," he said. "Be happy forever. If only—"

He stopped, entranced by the sound of a gentle snore. Claire was as natural and simple as a young animal that sated itself, and fell asleep, at one with the world.

Possessed by tenderness, he stroked her hair. He, too, was happy, in a way that he'd thought he would never know.

From some mysterious place a memory came back to him. Claire saying, "We don't really have any say, do we...like someone's pulling the strings and having a good laugh."

And he'd said, "Philosophy doesn't solve any problems. Only feelings do that."

He wondered suddenly if the feelings of love and passion, mixed in with protectiveness, that consumed him now, would solve any problems.

Or whether some nameless deity was having a good laugh. And if so, what about?

At dawn Claire was awoken by a distant noise. She padded out of bed and opened the bedroom door. Sure enough, the phone was ringing. Pulling on her dressing gown she left Randall sleeping and padded down the corridor to his bedroom, where the nearest extension was situated.

"Lord Randall, please!" said a female voice.

Claire drew in a sharp breath. There it was, the English "toffee" voice she'd so resented in Randall—except that he didn't really sound anything like that.

"Are you there?" asked the woman sharply. "Kindly fetch Lord Randall for me."

"He's asleep. It's early here."

"Oh, I see. Are you the housekeeper?"

"No, I live here. My name is Claire."

"Really. I'm the Honorable Honoria Gracewell. I expect Randall has told you about me."

"No," Claire said in a hollow voice. "He hasn't mentioned you."

"Never mind. This can't wait. I must speak to Randall urgently. I might have known there'd be a disaster when he went swanning off to the back of beyond."

"A disaster?"

"Well I certainly don't want to be related to Frederica Crossman. The Stantons do have a position to keep up."

"Does she make it hard for them to do that?" Claire asked tersely.

"She certainly will if she's allowed to marry Gabe McBride. Randall should be here to put a stop to it."

"Did you say—marry Gabe?"

"They're announcing it today, bold as brass. And the wedding's set for three weeks. I suppose she wants to make sure of him while she can."

Claire sat down suddenly. Gabe was getting married.

"Are you there?" Honoria demanded sharply.

Claire pulled herself together. But it took an effort to speak. "This Frederica Crossman—what's she like?"

"A widow with two children. Respectable enough, but not out of the top drawer."

"But how will you be related to her if she marries Gabe?"

"Because he's Randall's cousin, and Randall and I—this is hardly your business, is it? The point is that the Stantons don't marry nobodies."

"But Gabe isn't a Stanton," Claire said, a tad sharply.

"I suppose you've got a point. Maybe his wife doesn't matter too much, especially if he takes her back to Tennessee, or Wyoming—"

"Montana," Claire snapped.

"Wherever. But Randall's wife does matter. Eventually she'll be Lady Stanton, a Countess, holder of one of the oldest titles in England—"

"That's not what Randall says," Claire couldn't resist interrupting. "He says the Stantons are a load of jumped-up nobodies who bought the title a mere four-hundred years ago, and—"

Honoria's intake of breath was as sharp as a knife.

"Randall will have his little joke," she said in a tight voice. "Countess Stanton has to come from suitable stock, but I wouldn't expect you to understand—"

"Hell yes, I understand," Claire said. The twang in her voice had become emphatic to the point of parody. If this snooty woman thought she was talking to a backwoods hick then Claire would give her hick with bells on. "That's just what we say when we're breeding cows."

"I—I beg your pardon?"

"Suitable stock. Nothin' like it. 'Course you've got to know your bloodlines. We keep charts. Is that what you do?"

"I—"

"Hell, Gabe don't never buy a bull 'cept he knows his pedigree. Why, we've got one now, biggest thing y'ever saw, with the most eee-*nor*-mous—"

Honoria audibly gulped. "There's no need to go into detail. Just tell Randall to call—"

"No need, ma'am, here he is."

Randall had awoken to find Claire missing, and followed the sound of her voice, puzzled as to why she was talking the worst stage Yankee he'd ever heard.

"Phone for you," she said. Thrusting the receiver into his hand, she fled.

North, who'd just arrived sleepily in the stables, was alarmed to see her dash in, saddle her horse and ride off as if the fiends from hell were after her.

She rode hard until the ranch house was out of sight and far behind her. She stopped in a clump of trees, tethered the animal, and looked around for something vehement to do. She found it in a lone tree that stood fifty feet away. Snatching up some stones, she aimed them at the tree and had the satisfaction of scoring a bull's-eye with every one.

Then she sat down on a log and buried her face in her hands. What was she doing, throwing stones like a man? She ought to cry or something, like other females did. But everything about her was wrong. It always had been. She didn't know who she was or where she belonged. She'd learned all the wrong skills, and she'd never felt so much like a foundling in her life.

Gabe was getting married, and so was Randall. For she hadn't missed Honoria's silver-tongued message. They were engaged, near as dammit. She was blue-blooded, and "suitable" to be an earl's wife. A lot more suitable than a woman who didn't know who her Ma and Pa were.

She couldn't blame Randall for last night. Her desire had more than matched his, and she'd gone eagerly into his arms, meeting passion with passion, spurring him on, driven by an instinct beyond reason.

She'd had her moment when love was everything, and she would treasure it forever. But before her eyes rose the vision of the long years, filled with nothing because she was apart from Randall.

And apart from Gabe. And if only she knew which one of them she minded about most, it would be easier. Wouldn't it?

No, nothing would ever make it easier.

Six

Randall reacted to Honoria's news with a roar of delight, which affronted her even more. She told him so, at length.

"Hang on there," he said when he could stem her tirade, "Gabe's a grown man. He knows what suits him. If he's found the right woman at last, that's the best thing for him."

"The right woman? No name, and no money. You should come home and stop it."

"I'll come home when I'm good 'n' ready. As for trying to stop that crazy Gabe from doing what he's set his heart on—forget it. I'm not ready to die."

"Oh, really!" Honoria made a sound that would have been a snort if she hadn't been an "Hon". "You've always had a streak of foolishness, and he's made it worse."

"Either that or he's brought out the best in me."

"I don't know what you mean."

"No, I'm sure you don't. You don't really approve of me either, and you'll disapprove of me even more as I am now."

"Whatever do you mean by that?"

"Let's say I've rediscovered my roots, and not a moment before time. All that society life you like so much, shopping till you drop, dressing to kill, spending hours mouthing polite nothings to people I never want to see again—it's not for me. From now on I'm spending my days squelching through mud, breeding calves, smelling like a barnyard and loving every minute of it.''

"You sound exactly like that creature who answered the phone," she said in disgust.

"Yes, I do, don't I?" he said happily.

"Well, I don't know what's come over you since you've been there.''

"I'll tell you what's come over me, Honoria. I've become a cowboy. And you know what else? I enjoy being a cowboy. And I'm going to stay a cowboy when I get back to England."

"I don't like the sound of that at all," she said in a tight voice.

"I didn't think you would. 'Bye, Honoria. It's lucky we found out in time.''

When Honoria had slammed the phone down, Randall promptly telephoned Gabe. Instinct made him pick the dower house number.

"You old son of a gun!" he greeted him. "So you got roped and branded at last.''

"How do you know?" Gabe yelled. "I was going to enjoy telling you myself.''

"Honoria's just been on. She wants me to forbid the banns.''

Gabe roared with laughter. But abruptly he became serious again. "Does Claire know?''

"I don't—'' Randall remembered Claire's distraught face as she handed him the phone and escaped. "I think so.''

"She used to have a kind of crush on me," Gabe said awkwardly. "She's probably forgotten about it now.''

"Yes," Randall agreed, wishing he could be so sure.

"Can you make sure she's all right?''

"Sure," Randall said with more confidence than he felt. He met North in the yard. "Did you see Claire?''

"She rode off.''

"How did she look?"

"Like she wanted to cry and couldn't."

Randall got the directions from North and rode out after Claire. He found her after awhile, still sitting on the tree stump, with a mulish look on her face. His heart ached for her, but he knew better than to offend her with outright sympathy.

"What the devil was that accent for?" he demanded, sitting beside her.

"She thought I was a hick," Claire said grumpily. "So I gave her hick." She remembered that Honoria was Randall's as-good-as fiancée. "Was she offended?"

"No, she's just mad at Gabe, and at me for not stopping him. As though anyone could stop Gabe doing what he wants." He slipped an arm around her shoulders and gave her a hug. Claire let him draw her close until her head rested on his shoulder, and he ventured to drop a soft kiss on her bright hair.

Gabe was a fool, he reckoned, not to have snapped Claire up when he had the chance. Randall liked Freddie, but how dull she seemed beside Claire, who was fierce, thorny, sexy—and utterly adorable.

"That's right," she said with a sigh. "Nobody ever stopped Gabe doing anything. Nobody ever made him do anything, either."

"Otherwise you'd have made him marry you ages ago," he said. When she looked at him quickly he said, "I know, Claire. I've always known how you felt for Gabe."

"Made a fool of myself, you mean," she said gruffly.

"Will you stop putting yourself down? You're a wonderful woman, and I think he's crazy not to be in love with you."

She shrugged. "Freddie Crossman's got something I haven't. What's she like, Randall?"

He tried to remember. "Pretty, gentle…"

"Sweet and feminine?" Claire challenged.

"Well—yes—"

"Charming?"

"I suppose so."

"I'm not any of those things. I tried to be what Gabe wanted. I can rope and ride almost as well as he can. But he just saw me as his sister—or his brother."

"Does it matter so much that he loves someone else?" Randall asked sadly. "What about us, last night? Was I just a substitute for Gabe?"

"Of course not," she said a little too quickly. "But you don't love me either."

"Don't tell me how I feel. Claire, listen." He took hold of her shoulders and shook her a little. "You've got this fixation that you're unlovable just because you didn't get the man you always wanted. But did you ever lift your head and notice any other man? Did you give the rest of us a chance? This ranch isn't the whole world, and Gabe McBride isn't the only man in the universe. He just thinks he is."

She gave a watery, unconvinced smile. Touched, Randall caressed her face with his fingertips. "You were in such a rush to tell me that I don't love you. Did you ever think you might have that wrong?"

She shook her head. "Don't, Randall. You should have told me about Honoria at the start—before we—"

"Before we made love?"

"Whatever it was that we did."

"It was love that we made. You know that, don't you?"

She looked at him defiantly. "Does your fiancée know it?"

"My what?"

"The Horrible Honoria. She as good as told me you were engaged."

"Oh, did she! And you believed her?"

"She'd hardly have said you were engaged if you weren't."

"She's been saying it for years. It makes her mad that I won't say it, too. But I'm not in love with her, any more than she is with me. It's only the title she wants."

"I don't understand that," Claire said simply.

And she really didn't, he realized. Her directness and honesty were like fresh air after the society hothouse where he'd been trapped most of his life.

"Can you understand this?" he asked urgently. "I love you, and I want to marry you."

Something leapt in her, but the next moment something else held back.

"Randall, you don't have to wed me because you bed me," she said awkwardly.

"Is that all you think I— Claire, sometimes I could wring your neck."

"Great! And you want to marry me."

"Yes, I do, you impossible woman. I love you, and I want you to tell me that you love me. *Me,* not Gabe. I want you to say it was me in your bed last night." His jealousy rose up suddenly. "Go on, say it!" he shouted. "Say it was my face you saw, not his."

"How do I know when they're both the same?" The terrible words flashed out before she could stop them.

She could have bitten her tongue out. Yet it had to be said. Nothing in life had come easy to Claire. She'd never before needed to analyze her own feelings, and the effort confused her now.

"I'm sorry," she said, anguished at the sight of the pain on his face. "I'm sorry, *I'm sorry.* I don't know—yes, I do—I love you, Randall, I do, it's just—"

"It's just that you still love Gabe," he said bitterly.

"I don't know," she cried. "I've always loved him. When I heard that he was going to be married, I wanted to die. But when I thought you were going to be married, I wanted to die, too.

"I can't marry you. How can I be a proper wife, feeling like this. I don't know if I'm coming or going."

"And you never will know if you stay here," he said angrily. "Claire, don't you realize, Gabe is bringing his wife home? How can you stay at the ranch, watching them together day after day, torturing yourself—?"

"I won't. Don't worry about me. I'm not going to hang around like some damned poor relation. I'm good at what I do. I'll never be out of a job."

"Fine," he said angrily. "Spend the rest of your life drifting all over Montana with nothing and no one to call your own. It's obviously better than a life with me.''

Claire's eyes blazed. ''Well, I'll be all right. I'm strong, I can cope with anything. And I don't want you to marry me as an act of charity.''

''I didn't mean—''

''Drifting all over Montana, as you put it, will be a great life. I'll be *me,* what I really am, not pretending to be Lady Randall Stanton.'' She saw his white face and added more gently, ''That's something I never could be, Randall. I couldn't do all that fancy stuff, knowing what to call folk and where to sit them—''

''Rubbish!'' he said furiously. ''You can learn all that, it's just a veneer and it doesn't matter. What matters is loving someone and being at one with them—knowing they value the same things you do—like us.''

''Do you?'' she asked wistfully. ''You've been here six weeks. Maybe you've just lost your way. When you get back to England you'll find it again.'' She touched his hand for a brief moment. ''I think you should go home soon, Randall. It's been lovely, but we're just too different.''

''We're not different at all. We were born and raised thousands of miles apart, but inside, we're the same. Can't you understand that?''

Dumbly she shook her head.

His heart was too heavy to speak again and they returned in silence. Claire wondered if Randall was angry, but he was past that. He was brooding over his appalling picture of her life to come, moving on from one place to another, rootless, lonely, never quite belonging anywhere. While the man who loved her pined uselessly on the other side of the Atlantic.

As soon as he got back to the ranch he put through another call to Gabe.

''Hell, Randall? Haven't you got anything better to do than call me up? What's wrong now? Is my best bull dead?''

''Your bull's fine. I'm not. It's Claire. I'm in love with her.''

"Oh, boy!"

"I thought I could make her forget all about you. Hell, that shouldn't have been difficult." He heard Gabe's appreciative chuckle down the line. "But I can't."

"You mean you offered her the Stanton land and titles and she turned them down?"

"That's right. She turned them down. And me."

"Well, she always was prickly as a thorn bush."

"She damned well is not!" Randall said furiously. "That's just an act she put on for you, and if you'd ever bothered to look at her properly you'd know that she's sweet and vulnerable, and full of stubborn pride so she hates people to know how easily she's hurt and—"

"Whoa. Hold on there." Gabe whistled through his teeth. "You've really got it bad, haven't you?"

"Yes, I've got it bad," Randall said heavily. "This is one time the Stanton lands and titles are no use to me at all."

"Wait," Gabe said quickly. "I'm thinking."

In his mind's eye he was seeing two young boys, pricking their fingers, letting the blood mingle, and swearing eternal brotherhood.

From the ends of the earth to save each other! Which one of them had said that? Did it matter?

A glimpse of Freddie moving about the house reminded him just how much he owed his cousin. By sending him here, where he would meet the perfect woman, he'd saved Gabe from a life growing increasingly empty. With hindsight, he could see that.

Now it was time for Randall's blood brother to save him in return.

"Don't move," he said urgently, "Stay right where you are."

When he'd put the phone down he reached for Freddie. "Fred, how'd you like to go to Montana a little bit sooner than scheduled?"

"How soon?"

"Now."

* * *

Waiting for Gabe at Bozeman Airport, Randall wondered how he'd let himself be persuaded to stay over. He should have been on the next flight back to England by now. But, as Gabe said, it would have looked rude if he'd vanished before the happy couple arrived. He had a feeling that Gabe was manipulating him, but he couldn't work out how.

As soon as he saw them he knew that Gabe was subtly different. Some of his brashness had gone and he radiated fulfillment and content. Beside him, Freddie was brimming with happiness.

And the kids, Charlie and Emma! All over Gabe, acting like he was the greatest thing since sliced bread.

Randall kissed Freddie on the cheek and congratulated her. "Of course I shall expect you to go back and work out three months' notice," he said, straight-faced.

"Go jump in the lake," Gabe told him amiably, and everyone laughed.

But Randall had a strange ache in his heart as he watched them, so happy together. It seemed this kind of happiness was to be denied him.

Somehow they all squeezed into the sedan. On the way back to the ranch Gabe sat with his arm about Freddie, who watched, enthralled, as the scenery unfolded. Here and there the snow was beginning to fade, offering the first hint of spring and new life.

A new life for all of them, Randall thought, listening to the children's excited exclamations, and the contented murmurs of the lovers.

But not for him.

Claire came out of the house as soon as she heard them. Gabe was coming home with his future wife. This was the moment she'd waited for, dreaded, for years.

She saw Gabe get out and reach inside to give his hand to Freddie, saw the tender way he looked at her, and waited for the surge of pain.

There was nothing.

The pain came when she saw Gabe and Randall standing

together. Now she could see that their likeness was superficial. Susan had been right of course. Randall was far the handsomer of the two. Plus he had a gleam in his eye that could turn her insides to water, and a touch that could make her forget everything in the world.

She realized that Gabe was striding toward her, arms wide in greeting. She returned his hug, glad to see her brother again.

Supper was a big bash, with everyone there to meet Freddie and the children. Claire showed her around the house. She found she liked her a lot.

Nevertheless, Claire knew she would have to move on soon. She couldn't live in this house with Gabe, who would remind her constantly of Randall.

She went to bed early, leaving the rest of them talking downstairs. They wouldn't miss her, she thought. She didn't see Randall's eyes follow her until she was out of sight.

The next morning his bags were packed and he was all ready to go. But there was one last thing to do. He went to the study and lifted the phone.

"Randall, m'boy," Earl's voice boomed along the lines from England, "nice to hear from you. Gabe says you're coming home."

"That's right. Today."

"It'll be grand to have you back. Gabe's done a fine job in Devon, and it's given me some ideas for the next paper I'm going to take over—"

"Earl, listen to me," Randall interrupted him firmly. "I'm returning to England, not to the firm. Publishing just isn't in my blood, but the land is. I know that now. I'm leaving the firm and going back to the farm I rent from you. I'm going to be a hands-on farmer, and make the place the best in the country."

Earl snorted indignantly. "And I suppose you've got designs on the Abbey, eh? Want to be 'hands on' there too?"

"The Abbey belongs to you."

"No, no, a man should do a job properly if he's going to do it at all. You've got a contract with the firm. I could keep you there another six months. My condition for releasing you is that you take over the running of the Abbey. I'll leave everything in your hands. Never liked country life myself, but you prefer it, don't you?''

''I always did.''

He could have cheered at the way Earl had come up trumps. He was going back to his roots, the place he belonged. Only one thing was wrong. He'd found the perfect wife, both for himself and the way he wanted to live. But he wasn't perfect for her.

Claire hurried in. ''You're going right now?'' she asked.

''It's best. You know why as well as I do. I guess there are some things that aren't meant to work. Too much stands in the way, however much we might want—''

''Yes,'' she said, trying to sound bright. She was doing the right thing for Randall, she was sure of it. And yet...

''You won't mind if I don't come to the airport, will you?'' she said. ''There's a lot to do.''

''Sure, I understand. North's going to drive me in.''

''Not Gabe?''

''Gabe's too busy showing Freddie and the kids around. Claire—''

''It's all right,'' she said tensely. ''It's fine, honestly. Goodbye.'' Her mouth twisted and she added, ironically, ''Your lordship.''

''Don't call me that. There are no lordships between us.''

''But there should have been. You have your life and I have mine. We shouldn't have forgotten.''

''No,'' he said heavily.

He felt crushed by disappointment. Whatever Gabe had hoped to achieve by coming home, it hadn't worked. Claire's love for him was a barrier that Randall couldn't overcome.

He went to find his cousin. Gabe and Freddie came out onto the step when North drove up in the truck and helped Randall toss his gear aboard.

The goodbyes were stiff and awkward. Nobody felt at ease. Claire was the first to turn away and go inside.

''Let's go,'' North said. ''We're late.''

He slammed the door, and the next minute they were gone.

"So that's that," Gabe said with a sigh. "I had it all wrong."

"How do you know?" Freddie demanded indignantly. "You haven't confronted the real issue since we got here."

"*I haven't?* What about them?"

"Well, you can't expect them to be rational, can you?" Freddie pointed out logically. "Not when they're in love."

"So what am I supposed to do about it?"

"Ask her."

"What? If she still loves me? How can I?" he asked in alarm. "How can I go up to Claire and ask her a thing like that? I'll sound like a conceited jerk."

"What does it matter what you sound like as long as those two find each other before it's too late?"

"It's embarrassing," he complained.

Freddie smiled and took hold of his arm, looking into his face in a way he loved.

"You don't want me to think my man is a coward, do you?"

"Hell, no!" He headed for the door, then turned back. "But you stay close," he instructed her. "Just in case."

Gabe found Claire in the kitchen.

"Well," he said. "Happy now?"

Claire turned and gave him an artificially bright smile. "Of course, I'm happy. You're home."

"And I'm getting married."

"I know that."

"It doesn't…bother you?"

"Why should it? You're my brother…sort of. It's not like I'm going to pine away." She turned away from him then.

He stepped around so he could see her face. "Not about me, anyway."

She gave him a fierce glare. "What's that mean?"

"Fallen in love with Randall, haven't you?" His voice was gentle.

"Of course not."

"You never could lie to save your life."

"And you always had to be a big-mouth and spell it out."
She spun away from him again, but he came after her.

"Why not? Why should I let you wreck your life?"

"I'd be wrecking *his* life if I…if I…"

"Married him?" He slipped an arm around her shoulder.

Claire tried to shrug him off. "I'm *not* going to marry
him!"

"Why not? Don't you love him?"

She gave up. He was right. She'd never been able to lie to
him. "Oh Gabe, of course I love him, but it wouldn't work.
He thinks it would because this place got to him, but when
he's in England, he'll change back again."

"Will you let the man do his own thinking, for crying out
loud? He's decided that he wants you to be his wife, and who
the hell are you to tell him he's wrong?"

"But—"

"He's in love with you. But he thinks you're hung up about
me."

"*You?*" She sounded amazed, as though the idea had never
occurred to her. "Gabe, I've *never* been in love with you. Oh,
I might have had a bit of a crush when I was too young to
have any judgement."

"Thanks," he said with a grin.

A muffled giggle from behind the door told him that Freddie
was enjoying every word.

"But Randall," Claire went on, "he's a *real*—I mean,
there's just no comparison—"

"OK, no need to go into details. I get your drift. So why
aren't you on that plane with him?"

"Because he doesn't really love me, he just felt sorry for
me."

"There you go again, telling folk what to think. If you
aren't the most awkward brat I ever knew! You always were
and you always will be. God help Randall when you're married!"

"We're not going to be married."

"Oh yes you are!" Gabe said firmly. "I owe Randall a
favor, and I'm going to repay it. Now, some folks might think

it wasn't much of a favor to land him with you, but if that's what he's crazy enough to want, that's what he's going to have.''

''Oh yeah?''

''Yeah!''

''Don't you give me orders,'' Claire seethed.

''Fine, have it your way! Stand on your pride. Let him go. That man worships you, but don't you worry about that. Go ahead and waste your life and serve you right for being a stubborn, pigheaded—''

The next moment he was reeling from a sisterly slap on the cheek. But he was back in a flash, swinging her around and returning the slap on her rear.

''I hate to interrupt,'' Freddie said from the door, ''but are you two going to waste time fighting, or are you going after Randall?''

The combatants stared at her.

''Have we got time?'' Claire asked wildly.

''Leave it to me,'' Gabe said grimly. *''Move!''*

The two of them piled into the sedan, and in seconds Gabe was swinging it out of the yard.

''Don't worry, we'll catch them up on the road,'' he assured her.

''Will we?'' Claire asked anxiously. ''North was driving very fast. He said they were late.''

Going through the mountains, driving as fast as Gabe dared on the freezing roads, they saw no sign of the truck. Claire ground her nails together, sure that they would arrive too late.

''We've still got half an hour before his plane leaves.'' Gabe tried to sound reassuring.

At last the airport was in sight. As they drove in Claire saw the truck, with North about to get in for the return journey. Gabe screeched to a halt, and she almost fell out in her haste.

''Randall,'' she cried, running into the terminal. ''Randall!''

Far up ahead she could see him, just about to go into the departure lounge.

''Randall!'' Her scream carried the length of the building, and—oh thank God!—he heard it and turned, saw her.

"Claire!"

Randall began to run back to her. He didn't have to ask why she'd come. It was there in her face, alight with love, her arms open to enfold him and hold him forever.

He dropped his bags so that he had his hands free to seize her in a fervent embrace and draw her fiercely against him.

"You mustn't leave me," she said frantically. "I love you, I love you—Randall, you mustn't—" The rest was cut off.

"What about Gabe?" he asked when he could breathe.

"Who's Gabe? It's you I love. Only you. I knew that as soon as I saw you together. Gabe was a dream, and it was over long ago. When I thought you'd gone without me, and I'd never see you again, I couldn't bear it."

"All those things you were worried about—they seemed so important to you."

"They don't matter at all. The only thing that matters is being with you. I know that now. Tell me I haven't left it too late."

"It could never be too late," he said fervently. "I'd have waited all my life for you to come to me, because we belong together. I knew that, but you didn't seem to. Now I have you, I'll never let you go."

The final call came for his flight.

"Randall!" she cried in terror.

"Let it leave. Now I've found you I'm not letting you out of my sight. We're going back to the ranch for as long as it takes for you to get a passport. When you've got one, we'll go to England together, to see my grandfather."

He bent and kissed her again, gently this time.

"Then we're going to get married," he said, "and live happily ever after."

Epilogue

"**R**ight. Everybody hold it right there." Olly squinted through the camera at the sea of faces in front of the enormous Christmas tree. "You there, Charlie. Take that hat off."

Grumbling under his breath, Charlie removed the cowboy hat. But he scowled only until he saw that Gabe had taken his off, too.

"That's better. And you sit still, Miss Emma. We'll get them presents opened soon enough." Olly focused again. "Gabe, quitcher nibblin' on your wife's ear."

"Just trying to make her smile," Gabe protested innocently.

"You're trying to get me in trouble with Olly," Freddie accused, laughing.

"Well, he wouldn't be our Gabe if he didn't cause some kind of ruckus," Randall said tolerantly.

"Like you're so well-behaved yourself." Claire nudged her husband in the ribs. "Who was waggling his fingers behind Gabe's head five minutes ago?"

"I was not!" Randall protested, laughing.

Gabe gave him a stern look. "You're supposed to be the well-behaved cousin."

"I am," Randall said piously.

"Are not."

"Am so."

They looked like they'd enjoy nothing more than a wrestling match to settle the issue, so Freddie intervened. "You both have to be well-behaved now," she said sternly.

"To set an example," Claire agreed, "for the children."

Not just Charlie and Emma, but the new children.

"This year's crop," Olly called them.

The babies. Philip Randall Cedric McBride and David Gabriel Cedric McBride, the twins born to Gabe and Freddie in early November. And James Gabriel Cedric Stanton and William Randall Cedric Stanton, the twins born to Randall and Claire just a week later.

"Four of 'em," Earl said every chance he could get. "Who'd have believed?" His chest swelled with pride, as though he'd accomplished the feat all by himself.

Now he sat in center place, Randall and Claire, Gabe and Freddie, Charlie and Emma, Elaine and Martha all gathered around him. And on his lap, four babies.

"That's right," Olly said. "Now, smile."

They smiled.

Olly squinted, he focused. He lowered the camera again. "Earl," he said. "You're fidgetin'."

"I'm adjusting," Earl corrected. "I'm afraid I'm being— dampened." He cast a fond, albeit slightly desperate, look down at his four great-grandsons.

"Oh, dear," Freddie said. She reached for Philip and David.

"Oh, gosh," Claire said. She reached for James and William.

"Oh, good grief," Olly said. "This family ain't never goin' to have its picture took."

Finally, however, it did. The babies were dry again. Everyone gathered around again. They all smiled again. All except Earl who didn't just smile but beamed, his arms full of descendants, his heart full of pride and joy.

And then the gifts were opened, the turkey was carved, the cattle were fed and finally everyone but Earl and Gabe and Randall declared it a wonderful day and trundled off to bed.

"Don't be long," Freddie said, lingering on the bottom step to give Gabe a kiss.

"Count on it."

"I love you," she told him. "This has been the best year of my life."

"Mine, too," he said, and knew it was the truth.

In the kitchen Claire slipped her arms around Randall and gave him a hug. "This has been the most wonderful day. I'm so glad we came back for Christmas."

"Me, too. I wouldn't have missed it for the world." He kissed her hungrily, then reluctantly stepped back. "Gabe and I are going to have a whiskey with Earl, then I'll be up. Stay awake for me?"

He knew it was a lot to ask. James and William did their share of keeping Claire awake these days.

"Always," Claire promised.

He went into the living room and Gabe handed him a whiskey as he settled into one of the leather armchairs in front of the fire. Gabe handed another to Earl, then sat down opposite and stretched out his legs. He sighed.

"Worn out?" Earl asked. He was smiling. He never stopped smiling these days.

"Little ragged around the edges," Gabe admitted. "Be nice when the boys start sleepin' through the night."

"Amen," Randall said. He lifted his glass to that.

"They're a right handful," Earl agreed. "Two handfuls." He chuckled, pleased. "Did you see the way Philip was smiling tonight? I'm sure it was a smile. He's old enough to start smiling. David, too. I'd swear he giggled at me. And that James has got a twinkle in his eye. Right smart laddie, our James. Goin' to be a fine earl someday. And little William. His eyes follow me everywhere I move. I swear those are the smartest, finest grandbabies a man could have.

"You two ought to be thanking your old grandfather. Weren't for me you'd still be slaving away on all those newspapers, Randall. All work and no play. And you'd still be a shiftless run-around eight-second cowboy, Gabriel. All play and no work. So, what do you have to say for yourselves, lads? Lads?''

He looked from one to the other. Gabe's whiskey, untouched, sat on the coffee table. Gabe's eyes were closed. He emitted a soft snore. A glance in Randall's direction showed Randall doing exactly the same.

Earl sipped his whiskey and looked into the fire, and then at his grandsons. What a difference a year made. He smiled. Then he raised his glass to them both.

"To the finest pair of scoundrels a grandfather could have. Blood brothers,'' he remembered fondly. Then his smile broadened and he lifted his glass once more.

"To Philip, David, James and William. And, of course, Charlie and Emma." Couldn't forget Charlie and Emma. "Reckon you'll give your dads a run for their money, blood brothers—and sister—of the next generation.''

* * * * *